Flood Stage

a novel

KATE SCANNELL

Flood Stage

Copyright © 2010 by Kate A. Scannell

All rights reserved.

ISBN: 978-1-7325714-4-0

Cover design by Véronique Martinaud.

Published in the United States of America by

Word Haven Media, INC

Also by KATE SCANNELL

Death of the Good Doctor — Lessons from the Heart of the AIDS Epidemic

~~~~~~~~~~

This haunting memoir is an important addition to the canon of AIDS literature. Scannell writes beautifully and with an insight that escapes most physicians.
—Abraham Verghese, author of *My Own Country* and *Cutting for Stone*

Kate Scannell is the rare doctor who has been transformed by her patients. In this irresistible, informative, and enormously moving book, she tells not only her story, but also theirs.
—Gloria Steinem

An enormously moving, thoughtful, and compassionate memoir...
—Robert Armstrong, *Minneapolis Star-Tribune*

A remarkable book, part history, and part memoir that reads with the grace and eloquence of good fiction.
—Deborah Peifer, *Bay Area Reporter*

...one of the most startling and beautifully written books I've ever read from a doctor...
—Pat Holt, *Northern California Independent Booksellers Association*

For Diane Buczek and Norma Scannell,
whose lives flow with mine.

❖❖❖❖❖❖❖❖❖

Her full nature, like that river of which Cyrus broke the strength, spent itself in channels which had no great name on the earth.

But the effect of her being on those around her was incalculably diffusive, for the growing good of the world is partly dependent on unhistoric acts; and that things are not so ill with you and me as they might have been, is half owing to the number who live faithfully a hidden life, and rest in unvisited tombs.

—George Eliot, *Middlemarch*

Contents

baptism

MADDY BERTOLLI STUDIES her gnarled foot, a ghostly shape beneath the murky floodwaters obscuring her kitchen floor. Measuring the river's new rise against it, she says, "See, Trouble? Now it's up to the old scar over my ankle."

Trouble barks politely but doesn't flinch with Maddy's grim update. He simply stares at her while rubbing against her twisted leg, his pearly flesh glistening through the irregular lacework of his matted black fur.

Maddy bends over in her wheelchair and reaches for Trouble. She presses her hands against his thick flanks, squeezing out more of the Baptista River from his sopping back. Stroking his head, she tries to steady his quivering. She offers, "If you were one of those smart dogs, you'd take the high road out of here now."

But Trouble doesn't budge or show concern that his intelligence is being questioned. Maddy gazes into his cavernous brown eyes, imagining that she sees straight through them, into his small fist of brain that seems incapable of grasping the current peril. She gently lifts one of his ears to her lips and says, "You are my sweet dim bulb." To her chagrin, his unwavering fortitude shines a contrasting light on her own waning courage. Nuzzling his damp neck, she apologizes, "Forgive me, pal. I'm the dumb one here. This is all my fault." She draws him close and confesses, "I'm just feeling guilty about all this. But I'm not leaving our home, and I don't know what else I can do with you. I hope you trust that I'm trying my best."

Throughout the last week, prompted by National Weather Service warnings that the usually thin ribbon of the Baptista River had swollen to a fourteen-foot record height, she had deliberated over sending Trouble to safe ground on her Uncle Tony's ranch in Mendocino. But no matter how variously she had strategized, she could not conceive a plan that would convince her uncle to evacuate Trouble without insisting that she come along, too.

Patting Trouble's clammy flank, she wearily declares, "I'm afraid you're stuck with me, boy. It's you and me, trapped inside my pathetic story of—"

A muffled, faraway voice shatters her hoped-for invisibility. She jolts, and every muscle around her crimped spine clenches. She throws a hand over her mouth to stifle a scream while shockwaves of pain radiate out from a raw disc in her lower back. Glancing through the cracked pane of her kitchen window, she sees Bill Dunleavy in his black wading boots and blunt yellow slicker standing outside her cabin. He is transformed into a colorful mosaic through the irregular ruptures of glass.

"Damn!" she seethes. "Why can't he just leave us alone?" She hoists Trouble onto her shawl-covered lap where he shakes and spritzes her face. "Stay still, boy," she whispers. "Keep quiet."

She desperately hopes that Bill will retreat after reading the bold note she has tacked to the front door: "Nobody home! Go away!" That he, convinced she has evacuated her cabin, will feel he has fulfilled his self-imposed obligation to check on her.

Waiting for an indication of Bill's next move proves to be as excruciating as the angry nerves whipping her back. Trying to distract herself from both, she digs her fingernails into the palm of her clawed left hand. Her muscular right hand clamps Trouble's jaw shut. Privately, she bemoans the cold, sticky moisture that wicks from his body onto hers. But she remains perfectly still, fervently praying that Bill will bypass her home.

TWO DAYS EARLIER, when electricity last operated in the midcanyon, Bill had telephoned her to ask about her evacuation plans in advance of the impending flood. Although experiencing his call as self-serving and intrusive, she also realized that it presented her with a strategic opportunity to redirect his neurotic focus away from her. So, she concealed her irritation, thanked him for his concern, and labored to reassure him about her safety. "Please don't worry about me, Bill," she had insisted. "I've got rock solid plans. Uncle Tony is driving down here today to take

Trouble and me up to Mendocino with him. Really,"
she admonished, "you must have something better to
do than worry needlessly about me."

After ending the call with Bill, she immediately
phoned Ella Strather, the Sheriff's wife, who helped
her with household chores twice a week. She told Ella, "Now don't stop by today, because I won't be here.
In fact, my uncle should be arriving any second now
to take me with him to Mendocino."

"Well, it's a relief to hear that," Ella had responded. "Because the levee is going to break wide open
any day now! I just finished packing our valuables in
the pickup, and I plan on leaving tomorrow. M.J. will
need to stay here a while longer, being the Sheriff.
We'll meet up at his parents' when he can get away.
But can you believe all this, Maddy? Our little Baptista River is bulging at the seams! One of M.J.'s
deputies saw it from the rescue helicopter this morning, and he said it looked like a long dark snake that
swallowed an elephant. It's filling the canyon and it
looks like . . . well, like the end of the world!"

"The end of the world?" Maddy had teased. "Are
you using M.J.'s scanners to channel into the divine
now?"

Maddy had always listened politely but warily to
Ella's embellished views of the world which were often spiced with privileged information culled from
her husband's police scanners. While vacuuming the
floors or scrubbing bathroom tiles, Ella spoke in a
syncopated working rhythm, reporting news of wayward cattle and sheep roaming the canyon, the
Woods' constant domestic battles, gruesome local ac-

counts about wheat thresher injuries or silo fill accidents . . .

Ella had answered flatly, "Maddy, I'm dead serious. And I don't see anything funny about what's happening around here." In the not-too-distant past, her feelings would have bruised from Maddy's sarcasm. But having regularly listened to a celebrity psychologist who frequented Oprah's TV show, she had come to understand that Maddy's sardonic humor served as a "defense mechanism" that enabled her to cope with her dreadful physical disabilities. Enlightened by her cultivated insight into Maddy's flawed character, she had continued undaunted: "Maddy, this apocalyptic rainstorm is going to wipe us out. By all accounts, it's biblical. Over 160,000 cubic feet of water are gushing over the Choctaw Dam every second. And huge sections of the Feather River levee were breached just an hour ago! They say muskrats are burrowing through the clay dikes. And all that water? It's heading straight toward us! Our Baptista's already 16-feet deep, and M.J. says it'll reach flood stage at 25 feet any day now. So, my dear friend, if that's *not* the end of the world—"

"Forgive me," Maddy had interrupted, "but speaking of 'ends,' I need to get off the phone." She rapped her knuckles against the kitchen table and said, "Hear that, Ella? It's Uncle Tony knocking at the door."

"Thank god!" Ella exclaimed. "Because you and Ed are the only holdouts in midcanyon. M.J. will be so relieved to know that you've left. He's already so stressed out with all the pandemonium here—"

"Well, I do move slowly," Maddy wryly replied. "But you tell M.J. not to waste his time coming over here, okay?" She knuckled the table again and said, "I need to hang up, Ella. See you after the tides pull back."

Over the ensuing two days, Maddy tried to conceal all evidence of her existence from the outside world. To avoid being spotted inside her cabin, she ducked down whenever wheeling her chair past a window. She refrained from using flashlights or candles, despite the carbon black evenings enveloping her. She kept abreast of local weather reports through earphones attached to a battery-powered radio. And each night, she skillfully evaded detection by the Sheriff who shined helicopter searchlights over her property and bounced bullhorn evacuation warnings off her cabin's roof.

DEAR GODS IN HEAVEN, Maddy currently prays. *Please do not allow Bill Dunleavy to interfere with me now!* She shuts her eyes and fiercely summons her will which she hurls toward the heavens like a potent spear, aiming to pierce the mind of any listening god in possession of the authority to grant her wish. When she opens her eyes, she looks cautiously through the fissured window, checking whether her prayers have been answered. When she sees Bill hesitate in his path, a sliver of hope lifts her encumbered spirit. Looking conspiratorially to the gray heavens, she implores all on-duty omnipotent beings: *Come on—we all know it is too damn ironic for Divine intervention to visit me in the likes of Bill Dunleavy!*

While she waits for a decisive response, her amped up senses coil tightly around an expanding core of her anxiety. Now she is acutely aware of the stench of bloated cow pastures. She tastes acid in the back of her mouth. Her vision is assaulted by the kitchen's brutal demise. She hears the disturbing *shul-wulklulk* and *thuwaulk* of the swollen river cuffing the baseboards . . . the whining spine of a eucalyptus tree bending in the January winds . . . the eerie silence that has replaced her old refrigerator's usual cacophony.

And then, like a sonic needle, Bill's powerful voice punctures her tense hypervigilance. "Maddy," he yells, "you in there?" His tone conveys a revolting enthusiasm to save her.

"Damn!" she curses, her fledgling hope crumbling. Her rage expands in a feverish crescendo that rises incrementally with Bill's approaching footsteps. When she hears his rubber boots shambling across the porch, she bolts upright in her wheelchair, unwittingly dispatching additional pain throughout her back. "The indignity!" she complains to Trouble. "People think they fucking own you if you're disabled like me! They think they can just barge into your life and tell you how you—"

The kitchen door bursts open and Bill appears—a breathless, ruddy man slumping against the doorjamb, his red elastic cheeks billowing vigorously like dynamic blowfish. "Aha! I knew it! You're here after all!" he says with conspicuous self-congratulation.

"And you *shouldn't* be," she snaps.

"Well, what a lovely welcome," he manages, trying to catch his breath.

Maddy quickly surmises a risk to her master plan if she further antagonizes Bill. But feeling forced to stifle her fury makes her feel like a caged animal at the mercy of his able-bodied authority. She thinks, *I need to put him off-guard if I'm going to escape his neurotic need to rescue me.* Finally, she says, "I'd offer you a fresh lung, but the freezer's been out."

"That's a good one," he says, scanning her tousled kitchen. "And I could really use a spare lung now."

For an overlong moment, they stare at one another, waiting uneasily for the other's next move. At times, Bill's bronchitic gasping synchronizes with Trouble's panting, creating a strange harmony, a steely hew of metal saws.

The stalemate breaks when Bill scolds, "Maddy, you told me two days ago on the phone that you were evacuating this cabin. You *reassured* me that you were leaving with your uncle."

"Clearly, I did no such thing. Because you wouldn't be here now if you had *been* reassured."

"Okay, then—you *tried* to assure me that you—"

"Well," she frostily interrupts, "of all people, *you* should know how someone's plans can change sometimes, and without any warning."

Bill cringes while her trenchant comment bores through his beleaguered conscience. On target, it pinpoints his old cowardice that has hibernated for years within their strained past. It lodges at the intersection of their "before" and "after" which has located their relationship since her accident. In their "before," they had been inseparable friends whose closeness regularly fostered public speculation. They had been steady lunch partners throughout grade school, and summer co-workers in the strawberry fields. In high school, they spent weekends in the Glen Cove library, discovering Sartre, Dickinson, Salinger, Steinem, and Martin Luther King.

But in the "after" following her accident, they became awkwardly entangled strangers—two people incapable of letting go of a binding trauma, even as it weighted them down and dragged them into great depths of personal misery.

He nods to Maddy now, acknowledging her verbal potshot. If even obliquely delivered, it marks the first time that she has ever addressed his monstrous disloyalty to her. He accepts her rebuke like a soldier, silently bearing the reprimand for his conduct unbecoming. And still, he knows it merely grazes the surface of his deceit. It cannot inflict a sufficient penalty that will allow him to atone for his deeper betrayal—for the secret he has carried for decades that has drawn him toward Maddy as powerfully as it has driven him away.

Under duress of time and the press of the flood, he musters sufficient bravado to assert, "Maddy, I'll drag you out of here if I need to."

"The hell you will!" she says. "This is still my home. And I'm demanding that you leave."

He rolls his eyes upward to the same gray skies that Maddy had searched minutes earlier for on-duty deities. "Listen," he pleads, "there's no time to argue. I can carry you to Myrtle Road. Then the Sheriff can take you in his boat or helicopter to the Red Cross shelter at the high school."

Maddy glares at him, studying him as though he were a lethal virus, and wondering how to defend herself against his meddling mission. After an unsteady silence, she calmly states, "I'm staying here, come hell or high water—or come even you."

Bill shakes his head in disbelief. "You've got to be reasonable. The Baptista's just a foot shy of flood stage. We need to evacuate now."

"No, *you* need to evacuate my home," she says, wrapping her arms around Trouble like chains around a stanchion.

"Stop this nonsense," he says. "The canyon's filling up, inches by the hour. Look around you! Let's go."

"Save yourself," she says. "*This* time, it's *my* call. And I know what I'm doing. I've thought about this coming flood all week, and I'm not afraid. I've survived a flood every day of my life for thirty-nine years. This is my body, my life—it doesn't belong to you or any hospital committee now. I'm prepared— no, I'm *wanting*—to let Nature have its way with me. Pure and simple, no human interference this time around."

Trouble barks uncontrollably and Maddy tries to settle him down, to calm his old heart. Then he leaps from her lap in sudden pursuit of her red slippers that float through the kitchen, into the hallway and toward the living room. "He's got cataracts," she says.

"But what's your excuse for not seeing things clearly?" he shoots back, moving toward her. "I'm carrying you out."

Entwining her fingers around her chair's wheel rims, she shouts, "Don't touch me! You've got no right."

But he kneels into the floodwaters and tries to pry open her hands.

Maddy thrashes and rails, "Leave me alone!" The commotion summons Trouble back to the kitchen. He bounds toward Bill in slowed motion, hampered by muddy waters. In mid-bark, he clamps his jaw around a loose wattle of Bill's raincoat sleeve.

"Hell," Bill fumes, "you're both crazy! Tell your dog to let go of me." He tries to yank his arm free, but Trouble's jaw holds onto it like a metal-toothed hunting trap.

"Keep your hands off us," Maddy commands while Trouble's paws pummel Bill's chest.

Finally, Bill relents. "The hell with this. All right. Just call him off."

"Back away first," Maddy orders, her vocal cords straining. "Go stand by the door."

With Trouble dangling from his sleeve, Bill backs away, muttering incoherently. When he reaches the doorway, Maddy warns, "Stay where you are, Dunleavy. I can sic him back on you as easily as I can—"

"Seriously—*now!*" he thunders.

After gauging the likelihood of Bill's compliance, she commands, "Come here, boy."

Trouble emits a cautionary growl before releasing Bill's sleeve. After barking once more for good measure, he treads through the floodwaters and stands sentry by Maddy's chair.

Bill remains near the kitchen door, scowling, occasionally looking outside to assess the rising floodwaters. Maddy scrutinizes him, deciding, *He's imagining himself outside of his own character. And I know he doesn't have the stamina to sustain that much longer.*

During the standoff, Trouble's agitated jostling generates a watery commotion that liberates a trio of plump Florida oranges from the mouth of a burlap sack lying on the kitchen floor. The oranges ride a gentle current, passing a box of Idaho potatoes, the recently emptied wine rack, the buff-colored Formica table, and, finally, the doorway leading to the hall.

Bill implores again, "Please?"

But she only stares back, still analyzing their impasse. *He does not—and cannot—understand that I've had enough of my existence. He is vastly overrating my life.*

THROUGHOUT HER ADULTHOOD, Maddy generally considered herself oddly fortunate to have learned from her accident not to expect anything too compelling out of life. Life, she had learned, owed you nothing in return for any reverence or respect for it. And while you might be obliged to tolerate it, life—even one's own—was never "something to die for." Exasperating people like Ella who always claimed to be "intoxicated by life" only drank the good stuff. They knew nothing about the sober realities of life slogged out, one puny adversity after another, day to day. They could wax poetic about life's "great mysteries" because they'd never been forced to ponder the more trifling and pedestrian mysteries of a firmly earth-bound existence. They'd never been confined to wheelchairs and chained to duller daily enigmas—how to get to the toilet on time, how to retrieve the fork that slipped from your clumsy hand and onto the ground, how to wash your backside, how to muster sufficient will to make it through yet one more luster-less, mundane, two-cent everyday mystery to the next one. Naïve people like Ella were untested by adversity. And yet they always protested the loudest about life's appalling cruelty when a physical infirmity ultimately pinned them to the ground, forcing them to wrestle with minor mysteries that resisted all their saving abstractions.

Immediately after her accident at the age of seventeen, she had found these unbidden lessons difficult to absorb. But she soon discovered that the most efficient way to endure her new life was to accept it on its own indecipherable terms. She decided she would have to live it free of all expectations, without attachments to worldly justice or after-life rewards for her suffering. She would not yearn for any transcendent meaning of her predicament. And with this useful perspective, she could abide her life without fearing supplemental disappointments. Even when death arrived on its own unfathomable terms, it would arrive as a pedestrian event, as a humdrum disburdening occasion.

More recently, in the wake of the imminent flood, she had even derived comfort while fantasizing about the Baptista River swooping her up, carrying her away, and permitting her to drift out of life. At times, it was even soothing to imagine dying in the same river that had claimed her parents and aunt in the accident. Indeed, her own death by the Baptista's impersonal governance might even offer, finally, a healing symmetry to her life.

Since the accident, she had managed her existence with a few essential possessions that were made accessible inside the four cramped rooms of her cabin—everything she needed in reach of her wheelchair. Bags of Washington apples, loaves of French bread, and boxes of Italian pasta regularly occupied a squat metal cabinet in a kitchen corner. Nearby was the Formica table that her uncle once lowered unevenly with a hacksaw; it wobbled whenever she accidentally dislodged the "Niagara Falls, 1969" commemorative coaster supplementing the shortest leg. She cooked meals in a compact white microwave resting on a chair, and she washed dishware in a plastic tub that filled from an extension hose connected to the faucet. Years ago, she had commissioned her neighbor, Tomasz Podroski, to construct bookshelves that stood four feet tall along her cabin's beige-colored walls. A perky henna-haired woman from occupational therapy had fitted a bench across the bathtub so that Maddy could transfer from her wheelchair to the shower. In the end, everything she had ever required—in and of the world—orbited tightly around her, within the twenty-eight-inch sweep of her arms.

MADDY SHAKES HER HEAD at Bill, deciding it is impossible for him to fathom how, for decades, she has painstakingly constructed her solitary world inside the nine hundred square feet of this cabin. He cannot possibly understand how her universe begins in her chair and ends at her fingertips, and that all things beyond reach were mere surfeit distractions.

She says, "Bill, I know you mean no harm. And I even trust that you're trying, in your own way, to help me. But as difficult as this may be for you to accept, I really don't want to be saved."

Bill's jaw clenches, and he feels his knees become hollow. Fear and shame infuse his sensibilities while he is forced to imagine the prospect of abandoning Maddy—yet again—in another perilous predicament that strongly implicates him. He whispers, "You know I can't leave you here, Maddy. The river's already claimed six lives."

He surveys her face for a hint of consent, meanwhile registering how stern and pale it has become since their high school years together. He vividly recalls her face illuminated by the glow of a Bunsen-burner flame during chemistry labs, and her radiance regularly distracting him from their experiments. He remembers how miserably he had failed to rally the courage to invite her to the senior prom, despite days of fretful rehearsals in front of his mother's dresser mirror. And how, finally, on the Monday morning that he'd decided to ask her, he had paced around their lab bench, waiting for her arrival in class. How achingly those minutes had passed after the classroom bell rang and she had yet to appear. How stunned he was when Mr. Ellsworth ultimately entered the room and the students fell silent, waiting for him to speak. He remembers the agony upon hearing his teacher's unbearable news. That the Bertolli family car had slid off Berringer's Bridge and plunged into the Baptista River. That Maddy and her uncle had barely survived . . . that she'd been airlifted in critical condition to the Sacramento trauma center . . . that her parents and aunt had drowned.

Nearly every day since, he has re-experienced some remnant of the accident. He never forgets that he waited to contact Maddy for three full months afterward. And how, a blistering August afternoon, he finally shored his resolve to visit her at the Glen Cove rehab unit. In punishing detail, he can recall his arrival at the nurses' station with a sweaty fistful of white daisies, and the tired RN ushering him through chlorine-scented corridors to Maddy's room. When they neared her doorway, the RN stepped aside and, pointing a finger at Maddy, said only, "Over there."

But he froze when he stepped into her room and witnessed something more alarming than even his guilty conscience had imagined. Maddy looked like a hobbled stick figure, slumped in an oversized wheelchair on which was hooked a bag of urine. Metal contraptions braced her legs, and she was pinned everywhere like a rotisserie specimen. Her left hand was oddly twisted and cupped like a soup ladle. Drool trailed from her gaping mouth and onto her chin. The pink and chocolate crumbs from a Hostess snowball speckled her hospital gown. On her crowded nightstand, a chrome bedpan abutted against a water glass and desk clock. Her eyes were shut, and she appeared to be sleeping.

Potent reflexes immediately ushered him into an inglorious response he had not foreseen, one he could not tame with conscious effort. Instantly repulsed by Maddy's ghastly disfigurement, he abandoned his visit and his intention to tell her the truth about her accident. He dropped the white daisies onto the yellowed linoleum floor and exited her life for years to come.

BILL IS REELED BACK to the present by Trouble's renewed barking. He sees a red flyswatter drift toward the hallway where it bumps against the blue canvas air mattress on which Maddy exercises daily. A potted pink cyclamen bobbles nearby. He says, "Maddy, I won't leave you like this—not again."

But now Maddy is struggling to stifle her desire to lash out at Bill. She remembers all too well how he deserted her years before. How he had surprised her with a visit to the rehab unit, long overdue, and awakened her with his loud gasp in the doorway. How she pretended to remain asleep then, hoping to provide him a moment to regroup and muster a different reaction to her body's gross distortions and primitive failings. She recalls waiting for him to right his response, trusting him to seek her out within her own disorienting predicament. But, in the end, all he availed was an opportunity to escape.

Still, she is surprised by this first hint of an apology for his abandonment that has left her feeling ashamed and angry for decades. And though ruing this inopportune moment to confront him now, she realizes an opportunity to profit from his guilt and get her way. "Bill," she says, "I *know* you saw me in the rehab unit that day. I only pretended to be asleep so you could take a moment to decide, privately, what you really wanted to do after you saw the shape I was in. I didn't want your pity then, but I sure as hell didn't want you to discard me either. But I did see you, Bill. I saw you flee, and I saw those damn daisies on the floor. So, you need to understand that, this time, it's my decision—about whether you go, and about whether I live another day in my so-called circumstances. And I have decided—I need you to leave me alone, on my terms this time around."

Her comments sting Bill with their razor-sharp truth, adding to the burden of guilt he already carries. And now—as if his abandonment of her were not damning enough—he also knows that she saw him cower and turn away. The revelation further undermines his waning confidence, stripping him of any moral authority to demand that she accompany him to safe ground.

Watching rain leak through widening cracks in the kitchen window, he concedes to hopelessness about ever redeeming himself in Maddy's eyes. And he berates himself for doubting her two days ago when she told him by phone that she was about to evacuate her cabin. Had he chosen to believe her then—as his wife, Akiko, strongly advised—he would not be here now in this impossible dilemma, this degrading moment. He curses his dark intuition that compelled him to come. He curses the relentless rain that, still, will not wash him clean. And he curses his dead cellphone and lost opportunity to call the Sheriff to whom he could otherwise delegate his quandary with Maddy.

Recognizing Bill's mounting distress, Maddy strategically offers, "There is one thing you could do for me."

Bill looks to her as if entreating dispensation. "Anything," he says.

She hugs Trouble and says, "I need you to take my dog with you and promise that he'll be safe. He'll go peacefully with you if you hold onto him right."

"Please don't do this," he begs.

But her resolve prevails. She kisses Trouble's nose and says, "Goodbye, T."

"Maddy, this can't be right."

"Right as rain," she says, a half-smile forming. Then she drapes a checkered shawl over her dog and tells him to "be a good boy." After nuzzling him one final time, she hands him over to Bill and says, "You two go on now."

Bill slings Trouble over his shoulder, but he deliberates near the door, arrested by self-disgust. He knows that when he leaves Maddy's cabin, he also carries the oppressive secret that he never forgets, no matter what amount of whiskey. He searches desperately for something to say that might change his situation with her. But, like the floodwaters, his cowardice closes in, eliminating hopes for saving either of them now.

MADDY LISTENS TO THE RECEDING SLOSH of Bill's footsteps slogging through floodwater. Through her kitchen window, she watches Bill lumber through the canyon, the rain dropping in veils that partially obscure her view. Then she turns from the window and checks her watch, estimating how much time she may have before Bill reaches the nearest phone and warns the Sheriff of her intentions.

She maneuvers through the hallway and toward the living room, the solid muscles in her arms toiling to move her wheelchair through floodwaters now reaching her shins. She wheels past the air mattress and cyclamen, forging her way through a flotsam of fruit and magazines and cardboard boxes.

But arriving at the living room, she is instantly disoriented. "My God," she despairs, surveying her ravaged life. Through the combined handiwork of Ella and the flood, her living room has been transformed into an impossible arrangement, a watery nightmare erased of familiar landmarks and coordinates. Cola-colored floodwaters conceal the hardwood floors and create wavy tidemarks along the beige walls. Everything smells like moldy cornhusks and burnt cork. Books that Ella had neatly stacked on the sofa are toppled and warped, their engorged pages extending from their spines to form bulky paper accordions. Inside the brick fireplace, Trouble's toy bone is bobbing. The television roosts high on the mantle alongside shoeboxes stuffed with photographs and knickknacks. Two stout porcelain vases, a red-flowering Christmas cactus, and a glass-blown iris are repositioned atop bookshelves. The metallic grayness of the low-hung sky presses against the living room windows. A colorful striped T-shirt floats near the coffee table. Everything previously situated at ground level is uprooted and beyond reach of her arms.

She internally replays her original objections to Ella's offer of "help" with flood preparations last week. Watching Ella relocate the DVD player high on a closet shelf, she had drolly punned, "You're letting my life get out of hand." But fearing that overt protest might arouse Ella's suspicions about her burgeoning decision to stay in the cabin, she forced herself to watch silently while her uniquely articulated universe was dismantled. Still, every time one of her carefully positioned belongings was moved, she felt pain reminiscent of what she had endured after the accident whenever doctors reset her bones.

THERE IS NO PLACE FOR ME TO EXIST anymore, Maddy panics, absorbing her cabin's disarray and the terrifying possibility that, due to Bill's interference, she might be forced to survive this devastation. She sickens when she imagines Bill notifying the Sheriff. The prospect of having to recreate—let alone inhabit—yet another makeshift world of compromise poses an unfathomable proposition, a ridiculously exorbitant expectation. Her first gruesome resurrection at the age of seventeen—and at the bidding of her uncle and doctors—was trial enough; she does not need to prove her mettle to anyone ever again. She has abided for decades her miniaturized life without public complaint, reliving the same long day for almost forty years: the day she hurls through the windshield of her father's Rambler, tumbles through air, bounces off a concrete pier, hears her skeleton snap and crack, lies stunned and motionless on Berringer's Bridge, listens in vain for her parents' voices, begs for someone or something to extract her from her unbearable, pain-filled body.

No. I am not going through resurrection again.

With the floodwater now flush with her knees, she considers the convenience of slipping out of her chair, into the water, into oblivion. But she also worries that primitive reflexes might override her will and trigger automatic responses that prevent her from drowning. She is afraid she will survive in an even worse condition. *I need sedation—thought-ending, dream-ending, breath-ending sedation.* In quick relief, she realizes, *All the pills I've hoarded over the years! Finally, they might give me some genuine relief.* The pain pills, the muscle relaxants, the anxiolytics, the sleepers—collectively, they would guarantee an unflinching passivity through which she could slide from her chair and out of her life.

She wheels to the bathroom and pulls herself up by the safety bars. She flings open the medicine cabinet and tosses out Q-tips, floss cartons, tubes of unidentifiable ointments. Finally, she secures the vials of Valium and Vicodin and Ativan, and she falls back into her chair. The coolness of the air and river begin to penetrate the surface numbness of her legs.

But suddenly she realizes the awful irony in needing water to swallow so many pills. Though conceding that foul floodwater will soon fill her stomach and lungs, still, she cannot willingly drink it. She wedges the pill bottles between her thighs and begins her trek back to the kitchen where the bottled water is stored.

But when she enters the hallway, a deafening, percussive, crackling noise startles her to a halt. It sounds ominous and preliminary, like the initial crack of a massive tree limb falling, the telling snap of a long bone fracturing. An eerie silence ensues and encapsulates her. Anxiously, she waits for an identifiable catastrophe to claim the creation of the mysterious sound. She looks back toward the living room, scans the ceilings and floors, surveys the hallway. She strains to listen for telling clues, but all she hears is the Baptista River lapping the walls, soup cans clinking against the kitchen cupboards, the fuzzy reception of her AM radio, and the faint high-pitched creaking of a—*what*?

A thunderous explosion shakes her cabin by its roots. Objects resting on shelves vibrate and convulse before plunging into the river's violent groundswell. Family photographs somersault in the air like confetti and tumble into the opaque floodwaters. The stammering radio follows their lead and silences. Porcelain vases dive off the mantle like stout, clumsy swimmers. Maddy grabs the trembling arms of her wheelchair while flashes of frigid water shock her pelvis. The medicine vials lurch from her lap and submerge into the floodwater several feet away. She anchors one hand to her quivering chair and uses the other to dredge the waters for them.

Then the deafening explosion resounds, and she assumes that an earthquake has seized the cabin. The windows shatter in unison, and thick tongues of water stick violently through them. They unfurl toward her, instantly turn black, and she screams as the dark mudslide races toward her. She sees her living room wall swell like a huge boil that ruptures through its center, spewing tarry muck throughout her cabin. She pulls herself up along the doorframe and lunges onto the air mattress as the colossal darkness rushes toward her.

She squeezes her eyes shut and turns her head away from the gushing muck, bracing for a tarry death. Against the booming background sound of advancing mud, she wails. She wails from an unfamiliar place deep inside her chest.

The weighty black belly of mud lunges against her mattress and pins her against the wall. Suddenly, the entire cabin jerks in one enormous whipcrack jolt and then begins to move. It bounces and stutters along a downhill course. An awful, jarring thunderclap announces its arrival at the bottom of the hill where its boards and stucco and metal explode and burst into fragments. The roof pops off the cabin and cartwheels in the sky.

A thick lick of mud scoops her up from the debris but then drags her under its silted morass and flips her around. In the gelatinous darkness, she loses orientation and cannot sense direction toward the surface. She thrashes the air mattress back and forth until it frees from the muck. As she follows its lift, her shoulder bangs against something sharp, and she swallows clotted waters, part hill and part Baptista. And realizing the acute opportunity to be rid of her life, she almost lets go of the mattress. But the earthen water begins to lighten, and a deep current lifts her up and delivers her muddied, bloodied head to the surface. She chokes and gasps like an old car engine trying to start. Her neck flails with the jerks and bucks of the mattress against the torrents of raging river.

Not thinking, she automatically hangs on to the mattress and struggles to breathe through the floodwater clogging her windpipe. At first, she sees only colors—browns, blacks and grays. Things are formless if there are things at all. But then—floating trees and tricycles, puzzle pieces of buildings, trashcans, rubber tires, mounds of sodden cardboard. There is a wedding dress hanging from a tree. A car tangled up in the power lines. She readjusts her grasp on the mattress and sails past drifting cows, sofa cushions, a birdcage, a lampshade.

The river tumbles into the deepest section of the midcanyon and propels the mattress forward. She drops into the river's new chaos, sighting at once a row of eucalyptus trees the Frostee-Freeze marquee bullets of rain a blue trash pail a lounge chair a patio table . . .

She rides the roiling river as tremendous pain enters the same deep-throated place that her wail located earlier. The pain swells behind her breastbone. It pushes hard against her heart until it finally erupts into rage against her decades-long captivity within her caged existence. She throws back her head and sees the vast, dense grayness of the sky, recognizing it as the color of her life. She opens her jaw, stretches wide the back of her throat, and tries to let loose the keening pain. And when it finally escapes, it makes a sound not readily identifiable as human.

All around her, she sees the harrowing beauty of sky reflected in floodwater. Nearly four decades have passed since her body has moved so freely, and now she is rushing through the immense sea-sky, twirling and swooping with its unpredictable currents. She imagines her legs' insensate nerves reawakening as she leaps through the canyon, from one river rock to the next, her calves bulging with consummate strength.

The river pulls her past Ed's filling station. A pink sneaker bumps against her neck. She sails beyond the bridge where her parents and aunt were killed. A bundle of letters bound with green jute snags her mattress.

Now a cold, spacious cavity remains in the strange place from which she wailed. And up against its enormity, she recognizes it as the deadened core of her life, the hollow hub from which her arms have always swept to define her small circle of inhabitable world.

A spear of sunlight pierces the river. A milk carton glides by, a coffee tin grazes her forehead. She feels herself caving inwards, collapsing into the void of her untouched life. Its gravity seizes her as it also sucks in the leaden sky and the immensity of the river and the weight of her despair.

But then a loud fluttering noise claims her attention. An enormous, insistent sound that comes out of nowhere. It rapidly intensifies—a mechanical staccato, a stuttering in the sky. Maddy looks up but sees nothing. The sound recedes and is replaced by a din of voices and the rustling of wind through the tree lines. On the banks—a blurred commotion of red and black and yellow, of barely distinct human figures moving fast.

The river bellows as it funnels into a crevice between two approaching hills that a wood-planked footbridge once spanned. Now Maddy clearly sees people running along the banks, some of them pointing forcefully toward the hilly crevice while others gesture toward the sky.

The mechanical stuttering resounds overhead, and she sees in the near distance a man who swings in the air above the river, suspended from a helicopter by a thick black cable. Behind him, people wave to her from the inlet foothills, and the blue strobe of the Sheriff's car flashes.

But Maddy only feels distance. Solid, insistent distance. And the distance between her and the man on the cable, between her and the people on the banks—it is of infinite measure.

She perceives the entire scene as an illusion. As a fake backdrop painted with hills and water, studded with people arching toward her. And she imagines hearing the canvas rip apart when she passes through its center.

The river tousles her, and she nearly loses hold of the mattress. She spins around in the turbulence. When she rights with the erratic current, she sees that the cabled man is closer. He is shouting something while furiously moving his arms that extend toward her.

For days, she has steadfastly conceded to the river and submitted to the impersonal whims of remote gods. Throughout the rainy week before, with Trouble at her side, she obsessively reviewed her life, meticulously weighing the pros and cons of surviving the impending flood. And she concluded each time that, like the old accident that had defined her before, fate would intervene again—but *this* time with her assent, *this* time erasing its prior cruel workmanship.

The man on the cable gets closer, acutely narrowing any opportunity to reconsider her decision, forcing her to accept the choice she has already made. But envisioning her annihilated home and placeless life, she feels foolish for having hung on to the mattress for so long. She sees the rescuer loom larger in her path. Something punctures her flank. An enormous crow flies overhead. A strange orange fish with a twig in its mouth plops onto the mattress and slides back into the river. Shouts from the banks grow clamorous.

Then, in what would become the longest moment of her life, she sees the dangling cabled man ahead, his outstretched arms still beckoning to her, and she feels strangely buoyed by that aching void inside her chest. She sees on the riverbank the yellow frenzy of many vinyl-slickered arms extending toward her, too, whipping the air like golden windmill blades. And above the earthy roar of river, she hears voices shouting "Maddy!"

Suddenly the stunted roots of her arms stir, and they penetrate the paralyzed core of her life. Her arms lift from the mattress toward the cabled man, and, as they open to him, she feels them stretch beyond their usual span, toward the rain-pitching sky, toward the strangers on the banks and hillsides. The place of her old obscure ache pulses, its emptiness fills up with something new and radiant and alive that continues to flow through her as she reaches and reaches and reaches.

⌐ **when pigs swim** ⌐

I KNOW I AM A BROKEN RECORD about this flood. But I can't stop asking the same question: How could such a horrible thing happen?

Maybe that's because the only way to frame this unfathomable tragedy is with questions. All facts and answers fall short of satisfaction. Or they merely churn out more questions anyway.

I realize that good reasons don't exist for most of what happens in this mysterious world. Notice I say "good" reasons, not plain "reasons." Because there are always plenty of the plain ones to go around.

To my point—there is no "good" reason for a flood to destroy my home, this farm, my life and this community. For *every*-thing to become *no*-thing at once.

And I am convinced that searching all the world's libraries and churches would not yield even one good explanation to make sense of all this loss. So, if Ella Strather tries to inspire me one more time with another speech about the "redemptive potential" to be discovered in this flooding, I swear I am going to drown her in it. I'll be calm and polite. I will say, "*domo arigatou gozaimasu*," and then I will hold her head under the floodwater until, in my opinion, she is properly redeemed. And yet, she is so very durable. Chances are that she would survive. Yes, she would survive and probably become an underwater missionary. Poor, poor fish!

I am aware that I'm using Ella for a scapegoat. I suppose that's just so easy to do, especially when everything else has been made so difficult lately. Yet imagine me, just an hour ago, sitting on this fence and watching the Baptista destroy our farmland when Ella drives up—uninvited, as usual—and says, "Akiko, let's pray together. Let's ask the good lord for his forgiveness and love, to hold us in his strong hands and help us accept this flood . . ."

Well, I had to tune Ella out then because I had to concentrate on holding back my own strong hands that only wanted to strangle her. She's known for a million years that I am a Buddhist. And it's not that she simply forgets. No. She always wants to convert me. She even gave me a crucifix on a necklace for my wedding present.

But, enough about her.

I have spent most of my life—the life I'm losing now—here in Woodhaven, married to Bill, tending the pigs on our farm. And while I genuinely accepted such a seemingly confining life, as you might imagine, I occasionally got bored or depressed over the years. Though Zen failed to sustain me then, I discovered there was even more profound and overwhelming nothingness to experience through regular contact with pigs. There was more stillness in it, too. Sometimes, tending our pigs for hours on end, I barely moved. I was like a figure in a still life painting that no one ever saw. And then I'd look to the Baptista River and watch it steadily flow. It would move me and carry me along with it. I'd drift on the Baptista, which on sunny days became a watery mirror, projecting reflections of life everywhere. Mine included.

Another fact about pigs: they are not known to be terribly entertaining creatures. They are also not very interactive—at least in the usual ways. So, a person like me who spends day after day with them can go a little crazy sometimes. Frankly, I will admit that a person in such a situation might develop some strange ideas.

I figure that, averaging maybe four hours a day for thirty-five years, I have spent over 50,000 hours of my life with our pigs. And that's a dangerously high number of hours for any human to concentrate on a different species.

During those hours, I believe I have thought about pigs in every possible manner. I've dreamt about them, too, and that has only added to the odd repertoire of imagined possibilities. Pigs in checkered pantsuits. Pigs dancing hula. Pigs rapping tunes or riding skateboards. Pigs smoking cigars, playing paintball. You name it. And yet, not once did I ever imagine pigs the awful way I see them now: all hundred twenty-eight of ours floating on the river, like a creamy layer of pink soap bubbles.

I suppose this proves that pigs not only can't fly (except, of course, in my dreams), but they also can't swim. Unlike cows with their four air-filled stomachs, pigs are not aerodynamically fit for buoyancy. For that matter, they don't even walk that well. Their legs are so short and their hooves so narrow—they simply cannot carry their weight gracefully. Overall, they are products of a most unfortunate design.

And that sweet pig over there with the purple collar, the one stranded on that scrap of high ground near the footbridge? That's Millie, my favorite Tamworth, being pummeled by rain. Sweet Millie. It's so painful to see her like this, knowing I probably won't be able to save her this time. But I'm not leaving her without trying, despite the Sheriff's low prioritization of her predicament.

The first time I saved Millie was last spring. I was holding a cleaver above her squat little neck, ready to slaughter her for Easter supper. Then suddenly, she looked up at me so innocently, so trustingly, and she stared unflinchingly at me. I was awestruck by her absolute calm, and I was mesmerized by her seeming attempt to communicate something both to and about me that I ought to know. There was no separation between us then. I felt the strength of her faith—so pure and absolute—prevailing over mine. I believed that she was conveying a teaching to me, about fate and grace, about stillness in times of trouble. I just kept staring back until my arm weakened, and I dropped the cleaver to the slaughterhouse floor. I told Millie to run—to run free of me, and Bill, and her ill-fated destiny on our farm. And while she wobbled out of our curing shed, I vowed that she would never appear on anyone's dinner plate.

Bill was not happy—to put it mildly—with my decision to liberate Millie. When I served him sea bass instead of ham for Easter dinner, he brooded. He kept insisting on "pineapple-chunked ham" and the importance of observing "sacred American traditions."

But his protest didn't last long. Because all I had to do was repeat "sacred American traditions" while I walked to the dining room cabinet and stood by an old photograph of my parents. It was taken the night before they were incarcerated at Manzanar by our American government during the Second World War. (I still believe—although Bill denies it—that Bill's grandparents confiscated some of my parents' pear and walnut orchards while they were unjustly put away.) Anyway, I simply repositioned their photograph so Bill would have to see it throughout supper. My striking physical resemblance to each of my now-deceased parents only added to the effect I had hoped to achieve. I then returned to the dining table and wished Bill a very happy and scared American Easter.

And truth is, after his affair with Trina Woods last year, I also didn't give a damn about *any* of his appetites. In fact, I divided the Easter sea bass and served him the half that was mostly head and eyes, knowing he would hate it. But I told him that it was sacred Japanese tradition to honor someone with the fish head. And when he still hesitated to eat it, I calmly suggested he was lucky I hadn't beheaded and cooked up one of his whores instead. That silenced him immediately. Then I spread an Easter Bunny napkin across my lap and passed him the tartar sauce. This may sound unkind, but I enjoyed watching him suffer while he stared back at the cold black eye that looked up at him from his dinner plate. And I particularly enjoyed watching him discover how it felt when one spouse unilaterally changed tradition on the other. It was a most satisfying American Easter for me.

In fact, afterwards, I kept rediscovering that same satisfaction by upsetting Bill on other special occasions. (It's true what they say about the way to a man's heart.) So, on the Fourth of July, I served him a broccoli and mushroom quiche instead of chopped sirloin. I baked a halibut for Christmas. I made tofu patties for his 56th birthday.

Of course, I know my decision to spare all our pigs from the meatpackers was economically unsound (as Bill constantly reminds me). Especially after our financial circumstances suffered the 2008 economic crisis. But after my remarkable experience with Millie, there was no way I could send our pigs to mass killing factories. Whenever Bill gets upset with my decision, I just glare at him—the same way I glared at him when I confronted him about having sex with Trina at the town carnival—and that immediately ends his complaint.

I have known all along about Bill seeing other women throughout our marriage. After all, *we* were having an affair while he was still married to his first wife, Lynn. It's just that—well, he didn't have to be so sloppy with Trina and make the entire town aware of his philandering, too. He shouldn't have been so careless with her

I mean, at a public *carnival?* In a *tent?* He may as well have aimed klieg lights on the whole affair and sold a few tickets.

The real problem for me was that all our neighbors started talking to me about his tryst with Trina. They could not contain their need to discuss it, their zeal to make me conscious of it. Some of them even speculated openly, to my face, about the health of our marital dynamics! People began offering opinions and advice with a passion that only suggested desperation about their own marriages. The truth is, their constant chatter made it impossible for Bill and me to sustain the private understanding we had created to manage our marital frictions over the years.

You see, I have always believed that trying to talk with your husband about the things you don't understand about him only sets each of you in separate downward spirals. You just keep accumulating hard words between you that, no matter how numerous, never add up to genuine understanding. And you get stuck in a false mindset—a fantasy that someday you will finally say something that changes the other's feelings. But words too often become a humdrum habit between a couple, a substitute for real communication, so you end up using them in worn, tired scripts to say things you don't really mean. Then, in the sad end, you finally realize that all those useless words had actual weight, and, like stones in your pockets, they have dragged you both under.

Even if Bill and I had talked about our problems for twenty-four hours every day, I am sure it would have made no honest difference to our marriage. We would have remained the same tired couple still not having sex with each other, just a little more exhausted from having talked about it so much. And we would have said things we would have regretted forever.

No, it is not good to rely too much on words when you want to make sense of your husband or marriage. In fact, I have great respect for the healing powers of silence. And it is an excellent anesthetic. Besides, I really do not want to know everything Bill thinks or does. I do not need to be bothered with such useless information. And I most certainly do not want to discuss my private thoughts and feelings with my neighbors.

Bill is out in the canyon now, checking on Maddy. I don't know what goes on inside his head about her, but I doubt it's romantic or sexual. Still, she's always had something to do with his brooding nature. Sometimes, it even seems that she haunts him.

Back when Bill and I met—I was young, still living with my parents—I will confess that I needed to feel myself included within his raw carnal desires. I needed to feel that I could rouse and be roused by his dark, primitive passion. I am shy admitting this, but I was ushered into the urgings of my own sexual desires by the sheer force of his.

I love Bill for giving that to me. And after all the heartache he's created, I still want to wake up each morning and see his big soft body lying next to me. I want to hear him grind his coffee every day. At night, when he is finished working the fields, I want to smell his sweaty neck, watch him peel off his soiled work shirt. I want to hear our Labrador go wild while Bill chases him around the sofa after supper. I still need to see Bill look at me through his questioning eyes—an inquiring look that allows me to believe that I may also provide some answer for him.

Ours is a hazardous and complicated relationship. But our arrangement has served us well enough in the past, and the day that I start living my private desires according to my neighbors' expectations is the day that pigs will swim.

real estate

EVERYONE IN WOODHAVEN is worried about what they're going to do and where they're going to live. That's expected, of course. When a flood like this comes pounding on your door, there's not much else you can do but get out of its way and run for high ground.

Unless, of course, you're someone like me who can't fathom leaving.

All I can tell you is that paddling my kayak now through the *center* of town . . . it is so surreal and hypnotic. The land I once knew like the back of my hand has become an unfamiliar sea that no one's travelled before.

For the record, I'm staying here a while to help the Sheriff. I've been pulling neighbors off rooftops, rescuing chickens and dogs from cars and fences and what-have-you. I've chased away looters and freed dazed birds from oil slicks. God, I'm smack center inside the eye of an apocalyptic storm and looking out at the world through it! I feel as though I'm seeing clearly what Nature can conceive.

You might ask why a quiet guy like me would be drawn to such turmoil and devastation. I am just as stymied. This doesn't seem like me at all. And yet, I'm discovering that there's more of me like "this" every day now. I'm finding parts of me in all the wreckage, parts I never knew existed.

So here I am, adrift on shifting currents, sandwiched between the livid gray skies above and Markowicz's Food Mart ten feet below. Who could have ever imagined being suspended like this?

The only other time I felt so adrift—no water was involved. In fact, I was inside a bank vault in Michigan, at the Saginaw Savings and Loan. And I became suddenly unmoored while reading the letter my mother had left for me in her security box. She had been ill a long while and had died the day before.

Frankly, I had been expecting her letter to reveal the identity of my father, as well as provide information about her own estranged family. I'd been hoping to learn why they all abandoned us. I thought her letter might tell me where she had grown up and gone to school, whether we still had relatives somewhere or family that would account for my cleft chin and copper hair. I hoped to learn my mother's original last name, the one she replaced with

"Woods" when she fled from her mysterious past. I'd been waiting on all those facts my entire life, and I firmly believed they could fix me.

But her letter provided none of that. It did, however, reveal that she had "made a mistake with some boy" during high school—a mistake I took to mean *me*. She didn't reveal his name, and she offered no clue as to who he was beyond the fact of his enlisting in the marines after she became pregnant. Clearly, my mother had decided to take my father's identity to her grave. And I had mistakenly assumed that she had been waiting all her life to give me the opportunity to meet the man whose absence I'd been feeling all of mine.

She also wrote that I'd been the "best thing" that ever happened to her, and she regretted not living long enough to see me marry, to have kids of my own and "a regular family for once." She apologized for the nomadic life we had lived. She wrote, "Owen, I truly hope you'll know how to settle down at the right time."

So, when I finished reading her letter in that overly bright bank vault, I felt completely unmoored—losing with such thudding finality both the only parent I had ever known and my only hope of finding the other.

I spent the following week sorting through my mother's belongings and clearing out the small manager's suite we had occupied at the South Saginaw Motel 6. Even though we'd lived there five full years—a relatively long time for us to stay put—my mother had accumulated few possessions. One afternoon, while I was emptying our kitchenette drawers of sugar packets and matchboxes and outdated grocery coupons, the motel's owner stopped by to convey his "sincere condolences." He told me "what a fine manager" my mother had been and how difficult it was going to be "to replace" her.

I can't tell you how often I had heard those exact words spoken in relation to my mother before. Just about every Motel 6 owner in the upper Midwest had expressed them to her at some point throughout her nomadic managerial career. By the time I began community college, my mother had accumulated so many Motel 6 employee recognition awards that we just stopped saving them. Whenever she'd receive another, we'd remove the frame—if there was one—and set it aside for a garage sale. We moved throughout Ohio and Michigan and Indiana, from one Motel 6 manager's job to the next, guided by my mother's belief that it was unhealthy to be grounded in one place unless you were dead.

Anyway, it was disturbing to hear that motel owner refer to my mother in those same over-worn terms *after* she was dead. And stranger still, I found myself thanking him in the same tone of voice my mother always used to appease difficult customers. In the end, the owner shook my hand and left after requesting that I move my mother's Chevy out of the manager's parking space to accommodate its new occupant.

I don't remember much about the blurred weeks that followed. I have only a vague memory of—well, of feeling vague. For lack of imagination, I took up residence in "Club Rio," a sprawling apartment complex across the street from a famous water-pick factory in nearby Midland, Michigan. I earned a small salary working in the tool department at Montgomery

Wards. After a couple of months, I even met a girl at the Rio's social hour for singles. I took her to the movies one night, and afterwards, during dinner at the Red Lobster, she remarked how unusual it was to date a guy who talked so openly about his feelings and wasn't fixated on sports. I thought she meant that as a good thing. I also remember thinking that we had been having fun.

Later that night, when I dropped her off at her apartment, she thanked me for "such a nice date." I almost took her hand and walked her to the door, but I decided to go slow and save that for our next date. The problem was, she never returned my calls after that evening, and she even stopped attending the Rio's social hour. It left me feeling like an incredible loser. And if you had any idea how little there was to do in Midland, Michigan . . . well, you'd understand the dreariness of my situation.

My social life continued to take a downhill course. After spending several more monastic months in my bleak apartment—and ultimately distinguishing myself as the only employee ever demoted in Montgomery Ward's tool department—I realized that things *had* to change. If I was going to survive with any hope about the future, I had to leave Midland, the widgets and wrenches, the hammers and nails, the lonely luau nights at the Rio.

So, in the fall, I used my small inheritance to enroll in law school at a Catholic university in Detroit that was run by Jesuits. I moved to campus and spent my days in the company of brilliant, worldly men who talked about ethics and law, the meaning of existence, social justice and theology. My mind expanded faster than my thoughts and opinions could formulate. I addressed those men as "Father" and they always called me "son." And at some point, I began to feel that I finally belonged to a larger, more compelling world order.

Unfortunately, I quickly lost interest in the law. In fact, the more I studied it, the more unappealing it became. Classes became tiresome intellectual parlor games—students vying over who could best recite this law, that tort, one or another obscure ruling. Judicial decisions seemed to rest on unique circumstances and irreproducible details of particular cases, defying anyone's ability to apply sturdy, generalizable truths to worldly problems. You couldn't reliably use them to determine right from wrong within the next unique set of human circumstances. I found the law to be incurious and self-referential, and I was extremely disappointed by that.

The summer following my first year, I began a law clerkship in East Lansing with a circuit court judge. He was a strange man. He turned out to be a dopehead. Literally. The main thing I learned from him? Where to buy a dime bag from the best sources on the Michigan State campus.

He also taught me how to smoke, how to distinguish a merlot from a cabernet, and how to perform card tricks. And by observing him, I learned that all my life I had been buckling my belts on the wrong side.

The judge often remarked how much he enjoyed getting stoned with me. I liked it, too—at first. But I soon got bored because, whenever he got stoned, he'd tend to ramble on about his "brilliant" legal decisions and his self-proclaimed "visionary" judicial acumen.

He also tended to repeat himself because he'd forget what he had said. And sometimes in his foggy retelling, he'd even alter critical details of his cases.

I tried to space out when he droned on like that, and I'd focus instead on the music blasting from his massive stereo speakers. I usually sat to his left on the couch, turning a blind right eye toward him to make it appear that I was paying attention to him.

But one day, I had had enough of the judge. His narcissistic rants, his illegal activities, his shoddy ethics—they just aggravated my pre-existing skepticism about the law. And I had begun to feel like I had become a piece of furniture to him. It was late at night—only one slice left in the pizza box, and Janis Joplin singing about Bobby McGee—and I turned to him and said, "Your Honor, I'm leaving in the morning."

The judge had been talking up a storm, and my announcement barely interrupted his verbal momentum. Maybe he paused for a second or two, but I doubt that he registered what I had said.

Anyway, the next day I set out to find another job. After a disappointing breakfast pouring over the local classifieds, I phoned my law school dorm mate, Blake Maldonado, whose family lived in East Lansing, and I asked for advice. Blake suggested that I contact his father who'd been nagging him all summer to come up from Detroit and help with the family's restaurant business.

So, I phoned Mr. Maldonado that afternoon. He told me that he'd given up on his son and was happy to hire me to paint the A&W restaurants he managed near the campus.

At six-thirty the next morning, I was standing on an A&W rooftop, holding a paintbrush, looking out over the surrounding buildings while the sun eked above the horizon. I popped open a can of fresh white primer, imagining that I could whiteout all the torts, retorts, penal codes, and tainted judges that had settled as stains on my memory. When I dipped my brush into the primer, I felt oddly optimistic about the chances for my own life's renewal. And I found comfort in layering new coats of paint over weather-beaten boards, repairing old damages, making everything shiny again.

Mr. Maldonado was an egg-shaped man and a generous employer. All the waitresses he hired were undergrads at Michigan State, and the college crowds who frequented his A&W's were mostly entertaining. Still, after three or four weeks on the job, I became restless again. The enlivening metaphors I had discovered while working with paint began to fade. I stopped speculating about the meaning behind the mysterious "A" and "W." I grew increasingly intolerant of the restaurant's limited color scheme: brown, orange, white; white, brown, orange; orange, white, brown. And day after day, I faced the same meal "choice" from the same unchanging menu: hamburger, hot dog, root beer. My breakfast, lunch, and dinner were one and the same. Finally, when I dreamt that I was living inside a giant hamburger bun, I knew it was time to move on.

So, after completing work on one of Mr. Maldonado's restaurants, I thanked him for the job and told him I was leaving. He seemed genuinely sad to see me go, but he didn't protest my decision. In fact, he offered me a burger and root beer for the road—which I declined—and a good job reference for my future needs. We shook hands vigorously—for a few extra seconds, it seemed—and I walked away.

But as I was getting into my car, Mr. Maldonado rushed over. He threw his big sweaty arm across my shoulder and slipped a fifty-dollar bill into my shirt pocket. I resisted the money (and privately regretted the large orange footprint I had secretly painted on his roof). But he insisted, saying only, "You did a good job, Owen." Then things began to feel awkward when he choked up and a tear rolled down his beefy cheek. When he could speak, he muttered something about missing his son that made me envious of Blake. I tried to reassure Mr. Maldonado that Blake was temporarily preoccupied with summer courses, spending long hours in the law library. (I didn't mention that he was also studying a handsome Jamaican man who played drums for a local grunge band.) Finally, Mr. Maldonado wiped his eyes, slapped my back and said, "Take care, son." I drove slowly out of the parking lot, looking back several times to see if he was still on the porch. He was.

To my surprise, not more than ten minutes later when I turned onto I—96 for Detroit, I found myself craving a frosted mug of A&W root beer.

I must have been distracted by thirst because I next realized that I'd taken a wrong turn and was traveling instead toward Illinois. My first impulse was to take the nearest exit and U-turn back. But then I saw a billboard advertising a Motel 6 near downtown Chicago. And I felt Mr. Maldonado's fifty bucks burning a hole in my pocket, the momentum of his slap against my back pushing me forward. So, I just turned up the radio, and, with the Rolling Stones singing about getting no satisfaction, I reset my course and headed for that Motel 6.

Obviously, I was an expert about Motel 6'es. I knew they routinely offered reliable, rock-bottom comfort. They were accessible, serviceable, and predictable. As my mother used to say, "You don't ever go to a Motel 6 to be surprised."

But hours later, I was definitely surprised when I checked into my room. Someone had left a brown leather suitcase on the floor by the bed, bearing no identification tag.

When I phoned the front desk to report the suitcase, the manager only seemed annoyed. (Judging by her attitude, I doubted that she'd ever earned even one employee service award.) Finally, she said that if I *wanted to*, I could bring that suitcase to the front office. "Otherwise," she continued, "just leave it for the maid tomorrow."

I've never responded well to anyone's surliness, and hers made me want to be contrary. So, I hung up the phone and opened the suitcase. It was packed with men's clothing—two rayon shirts, a red and white checkered sweater, a pair of black creased trousers. It also contained a shaving kit, a first aid set, and a copy of *Newsweek* with "The United States of eBay" on its cover. After washing up and listening to the evening news, I rested on the bed with that *Newsweek*, falling asleep while reading about the troubled economy and the "new look" of Lasik eye surgery.

That night, I had a terrible nightmare. I dreamt I was trapped inside an extremely small motel room that had no doors, no phone, no electricity. The room was airless, and its dark windows wouldn't open. I began to feel sick and panicky. When I awoke, it took me time to realize that I was *actually* awake and *actually* inside an *actual* Motel 6 room.

I hopped out of bed and headed for the bathroom to splash cold water on my face. But I'd forgotten about the suitcase and stumbled over it, twisting my right ankle. I knew immediately that I had sprained it—having done so many times before. That ankle had remained vulnerable to reinjury after healing poorly with its first sprain when I was six years old. I'd been jumping up and down on a motel bed like it was a trampoline when my mother yelled, "Owen Woods! Stop acting like a hooligan!" And that really startled me, because neither of us ever yelled—it just wasn't allowed. So, I came down clumsy and hard, with my right leg slipping off the bed and catching in the sheets, my ankle twisting and snapping.

Anyhow, with my ankle once again turning into a boggy plum, I reopened the mystery suitcase and removed an ACE bandage from the first aid kit. After wrapping my ankle, I gathered my belongings, declined the complimentary continental breakfast in the motel lobby, and got into my car. I started driving west, intending to get away as far as possible from where I'd been before.

Despite my throbbing ankle, I drove almost continuously for days, often singing the song my mother used to hum about "California Dreaming." When I reached the Central Valley of California, I saw an exit for Woodhaven and took it on intuition. A "haven" for the "Woods" I remember musing. That was seven years ago, and the beginning of my new life here.

My mother, Patsy, would have liked it here. It's effortlessly beautiful country, and few "hooligans" live in Woodhaven.

It was strange moving here without her. She'd been my best friend for most of my life, and it seems to me now that despite her bohemian spirit, she, like me, longed for sturdy roots. Had she been able to come out here with me, I would have made certain that she'd never have to spend another day scrubbing motel floors, emptying other people's garbage, and laundering strangers' soiled bed sheets.

Most importantly, she would have loved hanging out with my daughter Grace and being called "Grandma." Like her, Grace has hazel eyes and wavy black hair, and she often hums without being conscious of doing that. Grace and I could have given my mother the opportunity to feel that she belonged to a family again—to something more than just the two of us had been.

Of course, my mother would have been disappointed to know about my divorce from Grace's mom, Trina. In fact, she would have felt responsible for it. Still, I know she'd be proud to see that, unlike my father—whoever he is—I didn't abandon Grace. Children should never have to suffer the childishness of their parents. And, despite my grievances with Trina, I'm making sure she won't be forced to scrub floors or struggle financially—because I don't want Grace to ever feel anxious about her mother's welfare.

It's odd, but when I arrived in Woodhaven, I felt that I had come "home"—even though northern California looked nothing like the Midwest. But the moment I first planted my feet on the ground in front of the Podroskis' bakery, I swear I could feel roots burrowing up from the earth, grabbing my sorry ankle, and anchoring me.

That first day here, I walked all over Woodhaven and never tired. I knew I was risking more damage to my ankle, but I kept walking. I picked up stones and tossed them into creeks, fingering low tree branches and pulling on cattails along the hiking trails. In the afternoon, I even climbed the soft browning hills that hugged the banks of the Baptista River. Near sunset, I explored a small vein of road that ended in a meadow bursting with blackberry vines. Flocks of wild geese flew overhead when I dropped into Thalburg Canyon at dusk. I inhaled strange intoxicating scents that I later learned to identify—jasmine, lavender, eucalyptus, cedar. I heard cackles and mooings and warblings that harmonized with the sound of my breathing.

Just before nightfall, I descended into the valley and stumbled upon a ribbon of the Baptista that trickled through the canyon. And all I can say is that skinny little river pulled me toward it with tremendous force. It made me stop and acknowledge it, communicate with it even. So, I lay down my sleeping bag on the riverbank and set up for the night. For the first hour or so, I stared at the sky and watched it ignite at sunset—a red-orange ecstasy that was far more radiant than the stack-fire lit skies above the Michigan auto factories. When I got hungry, I ate the two blueberry muffins I had bought at the bakery. Ultimately, the sky's brightness faded, and one by one the stars appeared like Christmas lights powered by the moon. I lay there counting them mindlessly, and, like a kid, I made a wish on a shooting star and fell asleep.

I awoke at dawn with the sun warming my face, and to a thick aroma of pine that smelled nothing like the pine-scented room deodorizers in Motel 6'es. I rolled up my sleeping bag, gathered my belongings, and traced my rivulet of the Baptista back to the small shopping center in the flatlands south of the canyon where I'd left my car. Back then, our "commercial center" contained only a handful of businesses: Markowicz's Food Mart, Handy Man Hardware, a Frostee-Freeze, Ed's filling station, and, of course, Arlene's Good Baked Goods—the Podroski family's bakery. And when you looked up, you saw Olivia's Bar on the highest hilltop not too far away.

That morning, I was the first customer in line at the bakery, arriving in time to catch a warm chocolate muffin and strawberry scone straight out of the oven. I ordered black coffee that had been freshly ground, and it was actually black—not brown like Midwest coffee. I bought a copy of the *Woodhaven Courier* and devoured its one-column real estate section. I was hooked.

Over the next seven years, I came to know every nuance of Woodhaven's landscape, its every geographic quirk, the exact dimensions of each resident's property, all the twists and turns of the Baptista River. I learned where the sumac grew, where the cows tended to roam, where tomatoes and strawberries ripened early. I knew where the high school kids hung out (in an abandoned trailer overgrown with vines) and their popular make-out spots near Olivia's. I collected old maps of the original farmlands that had been redrawn from one generation to the next. I could tell you about all the land "reclaimed" from immigrants, Native Americans, the Japanese during the War.

What's more, I parlayed my love for this land into a very successful real estate agency. And though mine is the sole agency in town, I attribute my success to *this* fact: I always aimed to find my clients a property that upturned their expectations and took them by surprise. That opened new doors for them, if you will. But it was never about "the sale" for me.

Unfortunately, I was never as successful with women. They've remained mostly foreign territory to me. I had no father figure when I was young, and I was older than most men when I began dating. I still have trouble recognizing when a woman is genuinely interested in me, or knowing whether she prefers friendship or romance.

Then, last year . . . Last year, at our annual Woodhaven carnival, I found my wife Trina having sex with Bill Dunleavy inside a carnival tent. I really hadn't seen *that* coming. And ever since, I've been haunted daily by the revolting image of Bill's blubbery backside flanked by my wife's legs. The worst part of it all was that Grace had to witness some of the drama from the sidelines. I'm pretty certain she didn't see anything "in the flesh." Still, as much as I had tried to protect her, she did see me turn wild with rage when I discovered her mother with Bill. Grace is a very sensitive child, and she had to watch me standing outside that tent, staring in, murderously eyeing Trina. That had to have scared and confused Grace, and I'll never forgive Trina for putting our child in that predicament.

And Bill—what an ass. I can't understand why Akiko tolerates his behavior. And I certainly don't understand what my wife—my *ex-wife*—saw in him that made it worth risking the dissolution of our family.

Still, if current truth be told, I'm grateful about what happened because it helped me to leave Trina. After everyone in town became aware of her indiscretion (thanks largely to Ella), I became a "wronged man" in the public eye. And I was granted communal absolution for divorcing her.

Trina had not been a "bad" wife before that incident. It's just that she hadn't been a good one either. Of course, I'm saying this in retrospect because, in the beginning, I had no idea what "good wife" or "good marriage" meant. Still, foolishly, I had believed I possessed both. It took me years to understand that I was merely co-existing with her in a tiresome fiction.

And despite my disappointments in Trina, I realize she is not a "bad person." It's just that, again, she's not a particularly good one either. She is severely damaged by her own fantasies about life. Just because you think free love is okay doesn't make it so for everyone else. And just because you think the world owes you a living as an artist, doesn't mean—well, that the world owes you a living because you say you're an artist.

I met Trina at Olivia's Bar on my second night in Woodhaven. I was feeling so full of myself then, invigorated with the newness of this town—its vast blue sky, its commanding hills, its animated canyon. And that's when she appeared, in a spaghetti-string T-shirt tight around her solid little breasts. She came up to me at the bar, tapped my shoulder, and asked if she could "help" me in a manner suggesting that she most certainly could. I was intoxicated—with her, some Jack Daniels, my new adventures in Woodhaven. So, we spent the night together, a great spark passed between us, and, boom! Grace was born.

These days, it's difficult for me to visit Trina, let alone try to talk with her. She becomes overly dramatic whenever she sees me. She cries and begs me to come back. She slobbers "I love you" repeatedly, in a way that strikes me as being rehearsed. Frankly, even if whatever she said were true, it would not convince me now.

While I still sometimes get moody over our divorce, I never regret our marriage ending. What I mostly experience is knuckleheaded disillusionment. I can't believe it took me so many years to figure out that what had been passing as "love" between Trina and me was little more than pragmatic partnering for her. What I thought had been actual sexual "passion" turned out to have been nothing more than surface accommodations for each of us. I had no idea that I was missing out on a genuine experience of romantic love—something I'd never known or witnessed before.

During our divorce, Trina said some ugly things. Once, while I was working at the office, she barged in and ripped one of her paintings off the wall. (She'd always hated it—an acrylic she'd painted for my birthday, of me in my kayak on the Baptista.) She was drunk and upset, and she told me that she had married me only because of Grace. She said that the sex we had had throughout our marriage had always been "uninspired."

That incident became a critical turning point for me. It was the second time I had ever experienced such potent rage, and its purity and force were clarifying. I had to admit that I badly wanted to punch Trina and knock the wind out of her wayward sails. I had to acknowledge that I possessed feelings I had always been reluctant to claim. And I would have punched her then if I hadn't remembered how terrified my mother once looked at the end of some angry customer's fist in a Motel 6 lobby.

Now, nearly a year after the divorce, I'm dating Suzanne Nichols. She's got a great kid, Tommy, who is Grace's age, and they get along famously. The thing is, Suzanne makes me unbelievably happy—which is precisely why I think our relationship might work. Because me being "believably" happy in the past was a downright mistake.

Trina got the house in the divorce—a solid craftsman on good high ground—because I wanted Grace to have a stable home with her mother. Last night, the two of them were supposed to drive up to Ukiah to stay a few days with Trina's weird brother. I'm still waiting on a call from Grace, to hear that she's okay.

It's strange to see Woodhaven as this watery ghost town now, especially having watched its population double within the short time I've lived here.

And, obviously, I know the future of my real estate business has become uncertain. But I'm not too worried. I made excellent money during the town's expansion, especially during the last invasion by wealthy Silicon Valley dot-commers who purchased as much real estate as they could. And later, when the dot-com bubble burst and they lost their quick millions, it meant new commissions for me when they scrambled to sell back their properties. Then—icing on the cake—I resold most of those properties at a peak of the California housing market, and I had little remaining inventory by the time the market crashed in '08.

Last June, I had the good luck—perhaps a real estate agent's honed intuition—to buy a small motel in Glen Cove where I've lived since the divorce. It is safe from the flooding here. When I moved in, I tore down all the signs identifying it as a motel, and I converted one room into a business office. I painted the building brown and white to make it less conspicuous from the highway, and I staked a redwood privacy fence around it. Still, it does retain some architectural semblance to a motel, and, on occasion, I've had to turn away people who came searching for a vacancy. That wasn't always easy for me to do. For example, just three months ago, I had to turn away some poor old guy who begged me for a place to stay while his mother lay dying in St. Catherine's Convalescent Home a few blocks north. He seemed desperate, and the jagged scar across his sunken cheek made him look defeated.

Grace loves to stay with me there. She likes to sleep with Rosie—her stuffed orange monkey—in different rooms on different nights, pretending that we are visiting different countries. We call it our "Motel 3." I'm still trying to teach her to memorize its address.

Woodhaven's landscape is transcribed on my body. It's mapped deeply across my heart and soul. And yet—this may sound like heresy—it is thrilling to watch Woodhaven's destruction. I am surprised to feel so much anguish for my neighbors while I also experience such euphoria over the flood. And while I am disoriented by the chaos, I am also being found.

I sit here in my kayak, like a drunken fool in the crazy rain. With the flood surrounding me and decimating Thalburg Canyon, I feel incredibly invigorated. I am brutally alive in ways I never imagined possible.

I see my neighbors' houses explode, rooftops somersaulting in the sky, mobile homes upturning or lilting like sinking ships, tractors toppling—and I am beside myself, craving for more. I watch the river knock down fences and surge over property lines, and I find myself cheering for it. The sidewalks buckle, the bridges spanning the Baptista shatter, and I cannot turn my eyes away from the magnetic fury of it all.

I am spellbound by this flood. I am mesmerized by its fatal efficiency and unblinking power to destroy anything in its way. Its primitive magnificence is electrifying—the uprooted trees, the ravaged buildings wedged against hills or dropped into sinkholes twenty feet wide.

I feel such a rush—watching bicycles, picnic tables, cars and what-have-you surge and tumble in the heaving river. I love the sound of the Baptista crashing against the hills, the cries of birds displaced from trees.

No visible canyon ground remains. So now the land that I have loved all these years has become a river that carries me to places I've never been.

I have never experienced anything more compelling than this flood. And I have never felt so wholly claimed.

⌒ what mom saved me ⌒

MY MOTHER GRABBED MY HAND—the one with the six fingers—and she pulled me through the woods so hard and fast that sometimes both my feet was in the air at the same time. She was running toward the river, dragging me with her, and I couldn't understand that. I mean, the river was flooding everywhere, and we even knew someone in our town who drowned in it. I kept screaming, "Hey, Mom!" But to tell you the truth, I don't think she even heard me. It was like she was under some kind of spell.

All the time she was dragging me with her, I was thinking to myself about how they was going to put pictures of her and me in the newspaper after they discovered our drowned bodies. And how they would write about us, like we was a tragic loss of a mother and son in this terrible flood. But they would never know about this real story happening—with us running in the wrong direction *toward* the river. And then I thought that maybe it was for all the better, because maybe my mom was going crazy sad, and this was like—you know—a kamikaze thing she had to do.

Mom really loved our little river that was all of a sudden big and flooding now. She always called it "my Baptista" like it was a special friend. I saw her lots of times just sitting alone by the river, staring at it. Sometimes I asked her what she was doing, and she would just say that she was spending time with her river.

She cried all night after the Sheriff told us we had to move out of our house for our own safety. And he was really mad when he came back a couple days later and we was still there. He said he would drag us out in handcuffs if we didn't pack up and go. Mom got the most upset I ever saw her in my life. She kept rocking back and forth in my dead grandma's rocking chair, saying over and over, very serious, "We are river people, Tommy." She told me that the river was in our blood, and that she was crying mostly because she was afraid that she couldn't give me our river life no more.

To be honest, I didn't understand what she was saying, but I thought I should remember it forever. And it made me sad to hear that she was crying about me, especially when I didn't understand why. But I was afraid to upset her even more by asking why I needed the river.

The ground we was running on was getting like tar soup, and I was afraid that my mom and me would be sucked into it before we got to wherever it was she was taking us. My legs was getting weak, but my mom's arms was strong, and she pulled my steps through that mud. She was holding my hand so tight that I was afraid she was going to pull off my extra finger—the little one with no bones inside. And it was raining hard, like there was huge faucets in the sky someone forgot to turn off.

Other people said before that my mom and me had a hard life. So, I thought maybe that was why my mom was dragging me to the river. But I never understood what people was meaning because no one ever told me why they thought we had such a hard life. It feels like a big secret. Sometimes my teachers look at me like they was sorry for me, and they give me bags of broken crayons or pencils that other kids leave behind. The Sheriff's wife always gives me a quarter when she sees me, but she never explains why. I don't really like people feeling sorry for me because it makes me afraid about what awful thing is happening to me that I don't know about.

My arm started hurting from my mother pulling on it, so I said really loud this time, "Mom! Stop!" She was so tall that, when I looked up at her then, it looked like her head was scraping the sky. I told her my arm was hurting, and so she took my other hand—the one with the four fingers—and she kept on running and pulling me through the wet grasses that came all the way up to my chin. She slipped one time and fell, but she stood right back up and kept on running. All I can say is that she was very determined to get us to the river.

When I was really little, I used to wonder if it was because of my father dying right after I was born that our life was supposed to be so hard. And while my mom and me was running to the river and maybe going to die, I had to wonder if it was actually me that made him die.

My mother used to get mad whenever I asked her about my hard life I was supposed to be having. And sometimes, she got sad. I was always afraid that, on one hand, I was being too much for her and, on the other hand, too little. I mostly tried to stay somewhere in the middle with her to try to keep her happy.

Finally, real close to the river edge, my mom stopped and fell on her knees in the mud. She pushed a big rock away and started digging in the ground with her bare hands. And she was breathing very deep and fast, and it was so cold that all this steam surrounded her head like she was true magic. Then she turned her face to me, and it was red and shiny like an apple from our refrigerator, and she was smiling in a strange way that kinda scared me. And I started to cry for her and for me, because we loved each other so much, but, still, terrible and mysterious things was happening.

But then she hugged me and said, "Tommy, don't cry! Everything's okay." Still, I knew that wasn't true, because we was in this flood, and we had to move out of our house, and my mother was covered with mud and digging the ground with her hands, and there was even a cow stranded on Mr. Archer's roof that I could see across the river. Things did not seem okay to me at all.

I heard sirens and helicopters, and the river thundered like a sky. I was thinking that maybe these would be the last things I would ever hear in my life, so I wanted to hear my mother's voice, too. I tried to ask her something regular that she could answer without me upsetting her, but I was crying too hard inside of me to think. Then she put her muddy hands on my cheeks and said, "Honey, this is where you were conceived."

I liked that new word "conceived." It made me feel like something special happened only to me, and it even felt good to have the mud on my face from my mother's hands. Then all of sudden she smiled very big and pulled a rusty coffee can from the ground. She handed it to me and said, "Tommy Nichols—this is yours."

I was thinking that maybe inside that can was my grandpa's gold pocket watch that everyone knew I wanted. Or maybe his old jackknife. I was very excited. I watched my mom's face streaming with tears while I pulled the lid off that can. Inside it was a stuffed plastic bag. My mom said, "Be careful when you unwrap it. It's delicate."

When I held that bag, I knew by its tiny weight that it couldn't contain a pocket watch or a knife. Then, with my mother calmed down and watching me like we was at church, I started taking apart all the Saran wrap bunched inside the bag. Finally, I saw something small and black that looked like a twig. "Be extra careful now," my mother warned.

All my fingers was so cold and numb that I couldn't feel the thing I was unwrapping, and I was afraid I was going to drop it into the mud or wind. My mother saw this, and she cupped her hands underneath mine to protect everything.

When I finally held what was inside, I was very confused. It still looked like a small twig. I held it up to my mother and asked, "What is it?"

She held me in her arms and cried even harder than before. She said, "Tommy, that finger is yours. It's what that drunken Doctor McCracken took off you when you were born."

Well, it didn't seem possible what she was saying at first. Because before, whenever I wondered about what happened to my little finger or dreamt about it, I always imagined it looking like a regular finger that just grew bigger every year along with the rest of me. But by the way my mom was looking at me, I knew what she was saying had to be very true. And then I thought about the horror movies that me and Gracie watched where people's heads got shrunken like hard leather raisins. So, I thought, maybe that's what happened to my finger, too.

Then I stared at the stump on my right hand where that little finger would've grown out of. And it was like my right hand suddenly felt happy to touch its little finger again.

"I have always felt guilty," my mother said. "I'm the one who insisted that the doctor remove your extra finger."

I raised up my left hand with its six fingers to indicate for her that this was the hand supposed to have five. She shook her head like she was disgusted and said, "I know, son. Believe me, I know. It was a big mistake. The doctor was in bad shape that night after drinking at his cousin's wedding. By the time your father and me realized that he had tied a string around the wrong finger on the wrong hand, well—it was too late. It was horrible. And I am so sorry, Tommy."

I looked at my mother, and I couldn't tell if she was crying now or if it was just the rain running down her face. But in that moment, she looked as beautiful and sad as a movie star in a very tragic story. Her hair was like shiny silver springs all curled up with the rain. Then she said, "Afterwards, when the doctor was going to tie off the extra finger that he should've tied off in the first place, I just screamed. I grabbed you out of your bassinet and held you so tight, and I warned him that if he ever touched you again, I would kill him."

My twig finger was crumbling a little in my hand, and the wind even blew a piece of it outa my palm. So, I cupped my other hand around what was left of it. My mother said, "I have felt guilty about that since you were born. Allowing that doctor to tamper with you . . ."

And then I could tell that she was crying for sure, because she grabbed me to her chest and it was shaking. She said, "I vowed to never again interfere with your specialness."

When my mother finally let go, she looked me in the eyes and said, "The doctor just wanted to throw your finger in the trash, like it was nothing, Tommy.

I couldn't bear it! It was part of you, a part I had no business changing."

She had to stop talking because her throat was choked up. I didn't know until then that my mom had such feelings about my finger. Whenever I used to ask her how come I got four fingers on one hand and six on the other, she just got very quiet. I didn't know that she was feeling guilty about it all.

Then suddenly, the rain started coming down harder than you could imagine. It was like the ocean pouring from the sky. So I was thinking that maybe we should get out of where we was because the river was getting huge. But my mother was still trying to say something even more important.

Finally, she said, "I picked up your little pink finger from the bottom of your bassinet. And I told the nurses that I was taking you home with me—*all* of you. They didn't understand, and McCracken just shrugged his shoulders."

I opened my hands to peek at my old wrinkled finger, and I was still having trouble thinking of it as part of me. But then something else was happening too, because it was like my right hand suddenly didn't feel lonely or empty any more.

My mother hugged me again and she said in her holy voice, "There is a perfect amount of you, Tommy. And I want you to live every part of your special life."

Then, I don't know why, I started to cry with her, and my mother smiled at me with a smile I knew I would never forget, even if she might get mad at me for something later on.

And then the river splashed us both in the face while we was hugging. For some reason, this made us laugh hard. My mother even threw her head back and laughed her very own laugh to the sky, and she looked so far away and so close to me at the same time.

So I kissed her on her cheek and said, "Thanks." But I wasn't sure why. I knew it wasn't just because of the finger that she saved me. It was for something else that I didn't understand yet.

She asked, "What are you going to do with your finger?"

And it was like I didn't even need to think about it. I just knew I wanted to throw my finger twig into the river. I wanted it to float by Miss Bertolli's house. I wanted it to touch the cow on Nick's roof. I wanted a big orange fish to swallow it. And Gracie's dad to fish him out of the river and show it to Gracie, and then maybe throw it back, and then a big whale comes by to eat that fish and swims to the ocean with it. There was so many things I wanted to happen with it.

So, I curled the four fingers of my right hand around the little black twig that I now knew was still part of me even though someone took it away from me once. I looked at it hard one last time, like I was taking a photograph of it with my mind, and then I threw it into the river.

When I turned around, my mother was reaching her hands out to me. And I don't know why, but I didn't grab them. I just wanted to run very fast all by myself through the woods and back to our house to pack some things to take when we had to leave. So, I smiled at her real big and I ran past her. I ran the fastest I ever ran in my whole life, and the rain was hitting my face, and I could hear my mother running after me.

But then I heard her stop, so I stopped too. And I turned around to see what was going on. She was just standing there, looking at me really hard. And she was kinda crying and smiling at the same time. I'm not sure, but I wondered if maybe she was finally feeling better about giving me our river life.

⌐ my life ⌐

ANNIE PODROSKI PEERS through the living room window and stares at her wedding gown as it flaps and gyrates under the gnarled cedar tree in the front yard. With each crisp pulse of the January winds, her dress steps lively above the rising floodwaters of the Baptista River. Hours before, enacting an instinct she did not fully understand, she had threaded the tree's lowermost limb through the gown's lacy sleeves and bid, "do widzenia"—good-bye.

Finally, she is ready to evacuate her home. The blue SUV that has served so reliably for her bakery deliveries now brims with remnants of her life that will accompany her today to Petaluma where her cousin, Sophie, lives. The single item she packed as a sentimental extravagance was her old red wagon with its bockety wheels. Nearly seven decades since she first pulled it through Thalburg Canyon, she can still feel the crude vibrations of its steel handle against the small bones in her hand. She can still hear its clackety racket of metal across the rock-strewn paths throughout the canyon. She can smell the warm mist of baked raisin, brown sugar, and melted butter from its cargo.

One week earlier, she told her friend, Ella, "I'm only taking those things that will fit inside my grave."

Shocked, and uncharacteristically silent for a moment, Ella responded, "That's awfully depressing! You should choose things that will fit into your *life*. You've still got plenty of good years ahead."

"Well," Annie replied, "when you actually get down to fundamentals, it's surprising to discover how unimportant most things really are. And besides, my room at Sophie's house is smaller than any grave."

ANNIE LOOKS DOWNSTREAM from her wedding gown, where thick flat thumbs of the Baptista River rub against the weathered footbridge she used to cross on her way to school. She is reminded of being the only girl in second grade who held a regular job and being envied by classmates for having parents who owned the popular local bakery.

She recalls canyon residents being reflexively drawn to the red-and-white canopied doorway of "Arlene's Good Baked Goods" on weekends. How patiently they waited in lines for the plump rye loaves that almost floated out of the bakery's ovens on Saturday mornings. Warm and heavenly, the bread's moist flesh stuck to the roof of your mouth like a sacred wafer.

On school days, she would awaken at six to pack her red wagon with standing orders from regular customers. She delivered baked goods to different sections of Thalburg Canyon on different days of the week, often venturing out beyond the flatlands. Her mother would wrap each order with a sheet of wax paper that she twisted at both ends— "making the pigtails," she would say.

Annie especially enjoyed her Tuesday deliveries because Mrs. Ladomerski habitually tipped her a few pennies and a paczek filled with strawberry jam. On Wednesdays, she regularly brought wheat bread and crunch cakes to the Dunleavys. Almost weekly, Mrs. Dunleavy asked, "Do you suppose your parents would consider making soda bread someday?" Thursday deliveries were her least favorite because she had to endure Mr. Markowicz's puzzling scrutiny. He would demand that she wait—*Poczekaj!*—while his stubby fingers unwrapped his parcels and he counted his biszkopty to confirm his receipt of a full order. Annie's mother provided her with only a cryptic explanation: "Henryk Markowicz cannot trust anybody because of terrible things that happened to him in Krakow. You must always be patient with him, Aniu."

During the Second World War, when Annie was seven, her parents took in a boarder from Ostroleka. Tomasz Podroski arrived on September 8, 1940, with one tattered suitcase and three English words: airplane, California, and help. He had been a master carpenter in Poland, and his miniature wood sculptures were regularly purchased by collectors around Warsaw.

Annie vividly recalls the moment under the old cedar when she first met Tomasz and shook his hand. It was thickened with a broad callous that bore fine branching cracks that had been darkened by walnut and oak stains. "Your hands are dirty," she said when she greeted him. "You'll have to wash before supper."

Tomasz smiled at her and said, "California." Then, from his coat pocket, he withdrew the small woodblock that he had been carving to bide time in the Warsaw airport, the skies across the Atlantic, the Greyhound Station in New York, the bus to San Francisco, and the taxi to Woodhaven. He handed it to her.

"Thank you," Annie said, palming the wood sculpture, quizzically studying the woman's face that had emerged only halfway from the woodblock. "But it's not done yet," she said. Tomasz's smile only broadened, and he again said, "California."

Every morning, Tomasz ate breakfast with Annie's family and conversed in Polish with her parents, Arlene and Pavel. Each day, after school let out, he kept her company while her parents worked the bakery. During their hours together, Annie spoke to Tomasz in English—about her geography lessons, her wagon deliveries, the perennial scabs on her knees, her wobbly teeth. In the beginning, he would only reply "Ah" or "Yes." But within weeks, he had mastered sufficient English to converse with her about jump ropes and tea parties and scab-picking.

Although seventeen years older, Tomasz quickly became Annie's confidant and friend. She loved having an adult companion who listened so attentively to her words and tried to understand them. At home, her parents insisted that she speak only English— "Polsku is not for America citizen," they always said. But increasingly, their own limited command of English failed to accommodate her enlarging vocabulary as it swiftly expanded beyond the commerce of family and bakery. Over time, by necessity, Annie and Tomasz created a blended language—part peasant Polish, part grade school English—that only they fully understood.

TURNING HER ATTENTION to the converted garage beyond the cedar tree, Annie re-envisions Tomasz in his green canvas apron, bent over his workbench, constructing elegant cherrywood cabinets and dining tables for Woodhaven residents. She remembers searching the Baptista riverbank for fallen tree branches that he often used to make toys for her. She was particularly delighted by the palm-sized dolls he created—each with a unique facial expression, and limbs that rotated around tiny metal hinges. They often played "statues" with them, taking turns to imitate each other's outrageous manipulations of the dolls' postures.

In 1951, when Annie turned eighteen, Tomasz requested her hand in marriage. He told her, "I never find love in Poland. I never know love until you." Her elated parents told her to accept the proposal. Her mother tearfully presented her old wedding dress to her, declaring, *"Aniu, mòje còrka,* this is right thing to do to make your parents happy."

What Annie remembers about her wedding day: That the sleepy-eyed priest sneezed into the gold-plated communion chalice. That Tomasz's left ring finger had been selectively bleached of stain. That her parents assembled an elaborate wedding buffet on the riverbank under the cedar. Tables were piled high with kanapki, dumplings, pieczarki, pierogis, salatka warzywna, babka and plum cakes. And, most note-worthy of all, she remembers feeling that nothing special or new was happening inside her heart.

Three days after the wedding, Tomasz moved his meager personal belongings from the garage and into Annie's bedroom that connected to the widow's tower off the second floor of her parents' home. Annie asked him to sleep on the rug, explaining, "I'm not ready for you in that way." Only weeks later, when he suffered with bronchitis, did she allow him in the bed. Still, she recoiled whenever he initiated any physical contact. Her body was not receptive to such radically different be-havior between them. And she felt neither passion nor instinct guiding her hands or lips toward her old friend.

One morning, months later, she awoke at dawn to a warm hollow in Tomasz's pillow. He did not respond when she called his name. She wrapped herself in-side their wedding Afghan and opened the door lead-ing to the widow's tower. There, in the far corner of its walkway, Tomasz stood, leaning against the wind-chafed white handrail, watching the sun rise above the tree line. "Tomasz!" she exclaimed, and, alarmed, she said, "Come inside. It's cold."

When he turned to face her, she saw a man who did not look like her old friend. His jaw was clenched, his dark brows were furrowed, his squinted charcoal eyes burned bright. He did not appear gentle or soft. She gasped at his strangeness. "What, Tomasz?" she managed.

He said nothing. But he continued to look at her while tears rounded his broad oval cheeks. Slowly, he extended his wide dark hand and held it open to her. She stammered, "What? What is it?" as her knees bent, her spine softened, her stomach fluttered.

He remained silent, staring at her so intensely that she feared she might faint. Her throat knotted, her breathing deepened, her chest ached, and she felt warm and commotional stirrings between her thighs. She stepped back toward the door, confused by her body's curious eruptions. But while holding his steady gaze, she felt his fierceness bending the shape of her old love for him. She felt the friction in her heart and soul as they rubbed up against the past.

When she searched for something to say, she was trapped in a wordless domain. Her mouth opened slowly with a new kind of hunger, her untrained hands began to seek what her new body desired. On the sun-beaten walkway of the widow's tower, under the fan of morning sun projecting above the East Ridge pines, with the aroma of bacon and onions wafting upwards from her mother's kitchen below, her heart dropped into her belly and then plunged into her pelvis. She felt her body move toward Tomasz, press against his flesh, erupt into one new ecstasy after another. She breathed his name over and over.

NOW SHE GLANCES AT THE DOORWAY that opens to that walkway and the stairs that she and Tomasz no longer climb. She is reminded of their fifty-eighth wedding anniversary last year, when Tomasz trailed red rose petals up the stairway, across the bedroom floor, and onto the tower walkway. There, he had placed a futon alongside a small table set with two brandy glasses and an expensive bottle of sliwowica. When she finally appeared after her workday in the bakery, she smelled of cinnamon and apples. Powdery white palmprints clung to pink daisies on her faded print dress, and her fingernails were blueberry-rimmed.

"Tomasz," she had laughed, "come inside. We're too old for the walkway floor now."

But he maintained silence. He poured the plum brandy and stared at her in the old way.

It had been decades since her knees first bent to his look on the walkway. But though stiffened over time and bowed from the weight of days spent standing before the oven, they yielded again. They slowly yielded, like a genuflection. Before the great mystery of their hearts, the miracle of their flesh, they whispered to one another, "*Moje życie*"—My life.

But the memory is unbearable, and she looks away, back to her wedding gown and the jagged currents of the Baptista coursing underneath it. She sees the river splitting into two separate streams around a small boulder, and she looks automatically to the horizon and envisions Tomasz in St. Catherine's Convalescent Home several miles beyond. He is tethered to a brown vinyl chair, dressed in a blue gown that ties in the back, spoon-fed by hands that work by the hour.

She remembers the precise moment of the stroke that separated them last year, diverting Tomasz back to Poland, and stranding her in a present and future without him. Four days after their fifty-eighth anniversary, ten-fifteen in the morning, midway through two eggs poaching. She was turning from the stove and toward Tomasz who sat at the breakfast table. She had been relating Ella's recent gossip: "So then, when Bill ran half-naked out of the tent, Owen started after him like a—"

But her eyes met those of a stranger at the table—someone who did not belong to their habit of morning eggs and breakfast conversation.

"Tomasz?" she had cried, dropping the spatula.

Over the next few seconds of bewildered time, Tomasz froze. Then, gradually, he thawed—his hands stirred, his face twitched, his voice churned inchoate sounds. When he finally righted his confused eyes and focused on her, he, too, felt as if he were looking at a stranger. The kitchen's buttercup wallpaper, its view of the vegetable garden, the steamy pan of eggs on the burner even seemed to disturb him.

Annie watched him leave. His eyes rolled back and became fixed on a time in which she did not exist.

"*Kim jesteś?*"—Who are you? he asked.

"No, Tomasz!" she pleaded, "Don't leave me."

"*Odejdź!*"—go away!

"English, Tomasz," she begged. "*Angielsku.*"

"*Nie mówią po angielsku. Nie rozumiem.*"—I don't speak English. I don't understand.

Annie searched her memory for the blended language they had created decades before, in the after-hours of school, inside their wood-misted garage. But few of the old words surfaced. She threw her arms around Tomasz, trying to steady him in the present. But the stroke expanded his remove, transporting him farther away. While she waited for the volunteer fire crew to arrive, he lay scrambling on the floor with his right side flaccid, demanding to be taken back to his Narev River home in Ostroleka.

After the ritual of blood tests and CAT scans and helpless looks on doctors' faces, Tomasz entered St. Catherine's Convalescent Home in Glen Cove. Annie visited daily, bringing him biszkopty, babka, or poppy seed kolaczki. She often gathered cedar scraps from the riverbank and red roses from their garden, and she placed them on the pressed-wood nightstand alongside his bed. She recovered her parents' Polish-English dictionary from the attic, and she tailored standard answers for Tomasz's cyclical questions:

~Yes, it is supposed to be warm tonight.

~I also prefer mahogany.

~I don't think you should drive to Warsaw now.

~I am sure your parents will arrive soon.

To his daily greeting, *"Jak się masz?"*—How do you do? —she responded variously over time:

~At first, crying, *"Jestem twoją żoną"*—I am your wife.

~Lamenting later, *"Bez ciebie nie mogę żyć"*—I can't live without you.

~Finally, after weeks, calmly responding, *"Bardzo dobrze, dziękuję. A pan?"*—I am fine, thanks. And you?

ANNIE HEARS THE SHERIFF'S HELICOPTER outside, a siren in the distance, and her kitchen faucet's aggravating drip that has become irrelevant *finally*. Glancing again at her wedding gown as it waltzes alone under the cedar, she thinks about time and the way it can separate people—like a river rock splitting a stream of water, sending one rivulet forward while the other circles back. Her heart constricts as she fully yields to her powerlessness to pull Tomasz back through time, to his arrival on her family's doorstep, to the tower walkway, to places where his tender heart found love. She imagines his renewed loneliness resurrected in his past by the handiwork of his stroke, and she feels her terrible longing for him in the present. But she knows they have become impossible reconciliations across the fractured flow of time.

THE HALL CLOCK CHIMES THE HOUR, signaling that she must hurry so as not to worry Sophie. And in this press of final time, she remembers the small woodcarving that Tomasz gave her when they met. She hurries to the bedroom and retrieves it from their dresser. She turns it over in her hands, examining it carefully, noting that the woman is emerging from it still.

"Tomasz," she whispers, fingering the carving, enfolding it in her palm. *"Moje życie,"* she says turning toward the door.

⌒ the seam between ⌒

IT HAPPENED SO FAST, it outpaced perception, it bypassed comprehension. The refrigerator lunged across the kitchen and pinned Doctor McCracken to the wall.

Hearing her husband's anguished groan, Tess yelled from the living room. "Alex? Are you all right?"

But his body was wedged between the Kenmore's steel door and a wall of stucco. A pantry shelf cuffed the base of his skull, and his old brittle neck angled sharply back. Only his right arm and leg escaped the refrigerator's press; they hung limp at his side and engorged fiercely with blood, dangling like plump sausages. Tess's fretful cries filtered unevenly through dense clouds forming inside his head.

"Say something, Alex!" she cried out.

Still, he could not speak. His windpipe was crimped, his lungs were compressed. Wildfire pain surged along every nerve. The glue connecting his body and mind began to melt, exposing the fragile seam between them into which he exiled.

But Tess called his name again, yanking him back into his tormented flesh and the unbearable present. The clanging of her metal walker against the linoleum floor prodded him back into awareness, forcing him to re-constellate around the brutal reality of a refrigerator pressing against his life. He tried to summon his medical acumen, honed over decades of practice, for self-advice about his confounding predicament. But any diagnostic insight evaporated the moment it materialized, leaving him dumbfounded about the increasing numbness in his legs, the revolting fire inside his belly.

The disturbing, rhythmic lurch of Tess's walker grew louder as she approached, renewing his besieged awareness. He worried now that she would stumble, break another hip. He wanted to tell her to slow down, to stop calling his name, to be careful and pay attention because their house was badly tilted now. But his voice could not rise above the kink in his throat, the rattle of kitchen chairs tumbling, the clash of appliances plunging off counters, the ruckus of room rushing toward him.

Stop calling me, he anguished. *I'm dying, Tess. Save yourself!*

A raucous quake shook the house again, and the kitchen floor buckled and dropped. Now water gushed in from the dining room, and Tess's walker silenced. Splicks and fizzles of electricity zapped the air.

The refrigerator pushed him harder against the wall, snapping even more of his old man's brittle ribs. He willed himself into the death that so clearly awaited him, but pain bolted through his body and fixed him again to his suffering flesh.

The sound of Tess falling against the wine rack drew him dully back into consciousness, glass bottles clattering in the rising water. He heard her sickening moan when she fell against his stunned right leg.

He tried to lift his head from the pantry shelf and bend his jangled neck to look down for her. But he could not even tell whether he moved at all. He whispered—or imagined that he whispered—her name. When his eyes strained downward, all they blearily witnessed was the river lapping photographs on the refrigerator door and the blue puffs of Tess's housecoat sleeves above the floodwater. Then a dreadful thud internally sounded when his neck cracked, his spinal cord snapped, and all stirrings in his limbs extinguished completely.

He prayed to be freed of his body and mind. Still, the tenacious seam between them refused to let him go. "Alex," Tess whispered, and, "My Tess," he wished to reply. Then the house foundation dropped again, and the Kenmore shoved him through the wall itself. His body's residual complaints about the floodwater's frigidity and the pain in his shattered bones quieted instantly. His senses faded, his vision gave way to darkness, his hearing became an unsteady high-pitched hum of failing nerves.

Then, like balloons released to the sky, the many facts that had tethered him to the world drifted out of his mind. The names of his patients, friends, office assistants and colleagues. Countless drug prescribing guidelines. Normal lab values. Cardiac support algorithms. Phone numbers for the hospital, the emergency room, the Glen Cove pharmacy. Vascular anatomy maps. Dermatome diagrams. Mnemonics for . . .

And the weight of a thousand agonies began lifting from his heart. The Bertolli family carnage off Berringer's Bridge. Maddy, bent and broken and pleading for death. The Rodriguez baby, lifeless in her crib. Henryk Markowicz's decayed body discovered in the basement. Ed Utley's botched cataract. A newborn's healthy finger dangling from a string.

And now . . . He sits with Tess on the Baptista riverbank, and she is placing a silencing finger on his lips as he begins to confess about the nurse in Glen Cove. Now, they are in the bedroom with their stillborn lying between them on a bloodied sheet, Tess reaching for him. Now, Tess is lathering his chin and scraping a razor across it, encouraging him to dress and eat, waiting for him to move beyond his paralyzing guilt over a patient's botched surgery.

When his life finally slips beyond the spectrum of awareness, what only remains is Tess's steady look into his eyes—her searching expression that could always find him before.

⌐ all right enough ⌐

I MOVED TO WOODHAVEN hoping to disappear. To vanish—*poof!*—slip off the world's radar unseen. And not in any symbolic sense, mind you.

At a minimum, I had hoped to find a place that would take no real notice of me. Because all I wanted after my husband Leonard died was to sleep through the rest of my life and wake up released from it.

But that is not how things turned out for me.

I have held different theories about what happened instead over the near-fifty years I ended up living here. And like most people, I've occasionally edited my memory to support my various theories. Because some-times you just *have* to shove a fact or two aside to be able to move forward to the next moment in life. Still, there's one steady truth that survived *all* my editing of the past—my husband Leonard.

When I moved here in 1959 after he died, I was in total ruin. Completely devitalized and unable to shift out of my happy past with him. I tried so hard to get unstuck and move on. And once in a great while, I experienced brief moments of believing I would succeed. But I had to work *nonstop* to make those moments happen. I just wore myself down *trying* to live without Leonard.

While he was alive, my days had been trying enough—with my full-time job and the commuting it required, on top of the daily routines of getting by that everyone endures. But after he passed, the simplest of things—things that seem so unremarkable or automatic—they became outright challenges for me. For example, just sitting on the couch—now that may sound unexceptional and unproblematic. But I swear, after Leonard died, I couldn't "just sit" on the couch any longer. Because when I sat on our couch, I had to sit there *without* him. That required me to perform a new act in totally different circumstances. You see, I had to sit there *without* his big hand resting on my knee, *without* the sound of his perpetual sneezing, *without* him torturing me with his stinky feet on my lap, *without* him always whispering "Sweetheart" in my ear.

Spending all my energy trying to be without him left me with no energy to simply be. And trying so hard to pay no attention to what I no longer had, I ended up not paying attention to what was actually happening. All the while I struggled to loosen myself from the past and pay overdue attention to the present, I also had to force my-self into a bleak future without Leonard. My life became unlivable along any sane timeline. It became defined solely by my timeless love and longing for Leonard.

Things got crazy sometimes, with everything either fixed in the past or imagined in the future. I'd show up for church on the wrong days. The garbage cans overfilled too many times. Twice, my electricity was shut off when I forgot to pay the bill, and I had to explain my sorry predicament to disinterested strangers at PG&E.

You can see how this situation was unhealthy for me.

I had visited Woodhaven by accident a couple of years before Leonard's death. Back then, I was working for the Public Utilities Commission, inspecting water companies throughout Northern California. That required me to spend a night away from Leonard about twice a month. But that wasn't so bad, because we always made the most of my returns home. (He was very romantic.) Besides, I liked my job. It provided good income and interesting work. And it was prize employment for a black woman then—really, for any woman in the 1950s.

So, one day, the Chrysler broke down on my way to a water utility inspection in Yuba City. Fortunate-ly, I remembered seeing a road sign about a mile back that read, "Gas and Food." I got out of the car, gathered my overnight bag from the trunk, and trudged back down that unpaved road while the sun blazed overhead. All the while, a disquieting country song about outlaw cowboys roaming the wilderness replayed inside my head.

By the time I reached the so-called service station, my face and legs were coated with gray road dust, and my long cotton dress was soaked with sweat. And what I mostly saw were sky-high heaps of discarded cars and rusted auto parts. Tacked onto a small gas pump was a sheet of butcher-block paper on which someone had written the price of the gas. There was a hand-painted sign on the door of the lopsided station that read: "Enter at Your Own Risk—Mechanic Inside." I called out "hello," but no one responded. All I heard were cats clawing the upholstery on junked car seats.

My situation felt sinister. As the minutes passed, I grew increasingly anxious. Yet, as dehydrated as I was, tears flowed down my face.

I began to panic, fearing that I had become stranded in one of those backwoods boonies that regularly provided hiding place for the corpses of missing persons. I kept calling out for help while trying to fend off images of rednecks tossing my future dead self onto a heap of auto carcasses, leaving me to the wants of beady-eyed vultures.

Then, out of nowhere, a hand fell on my shoulder. I screamed and nearly had a heart attack. I turned around with my fists raised and prepared to fight, only to see a spindly old man standing there, grinning at me.

He tried to calm me down. But all the while, a glint in his fleshy eyes made me suspect that he was enjoying his success in startling me. I wondered if he was trying to intimidate me simply because I was black, because I was a woman, because I was conspicuously alone. My suspicions deepened when he asked me to imitate the sounds that my Chrysler made before it died on the road. I thought he was trying to make me look and sound the fool.

Still, I was trapped. I scanned my surroundings to strategize where I could run if I needed to escape. I fisted my hand around my car key, preparing to poke out his glinty eyes if I had to. And, mentally primed for flight, I imitated the sputtery, giving-it-up sounds of my Chrysler. I repeated them once at his insistence, waiting with excruciating vigilance for him to declare his telling next move. All the while, the car key's metal teeth gnawed my sweaty palm, and my throat burned with dry heat.

But for a long while, he just nodded and fingered a tarnished crucifix that poked through a hole in his threadbare T-shirt. Finally, he stroked his stubbled chin and, looking to the cloudless sky, declared in a calm squeaky voice: "It'll take me one or two days to get the parts."

A new fear took hold of me. I couldn't figure out if he was telling the truth, and one or two days seemed too long a time to be at some stranger's mercy. I wondered if he was trying to make me feel helpless, and I was overcome by paranoia and indecision.

Then he said something odd that threw me off guard. After flashing me a sidelong, mercury-filled grin, he proclaimed, "Praise all of God's children and give them wheels."

I didn't understand his remark. On the surface, it seemed innocent enough. Still, I was keenly aware of the cruel and gruesome things that people could do while praising their various gods.

So I said nothing but stayed alert, preparing to flee. And I tried not to flinch when he too authoritatively declared that I'd be staying the night in a room above the town's local bar. Before I could challenge his decree, he had picked up my overnight bag and headed toward the same clearing in the backwoods that I had marked for my escape. I was reluctant to follow him. I feared he could be leading me to some den of torture, filled with bloated greasy men petting sawed-off shotguns.

But I followed him because I saw no other option. Still, all the while, I kept a safe distance between us and held on to a speck of dumb hope that he might help me. We trekked up one hill and down another, walked past a bakery with red and white awnings, trudged alongside a thin creek with a river's name, and crossed a droopy wooden footbridge to the opposite bank. Along our route, that little man whistled while I stayed vigilant for any hint of tragic consequences awaiting me.

Finally, we arrived at the foot of the highest hill in Thalburg Canyon. I was completely wilted, and the back of my neck was burning from so much sun. And then, to my amazement, the strange little man turned to me and said, "My name is Ed Utley." Before I could reply, he pointed to the hill's crest and began scrambling toward it. He climbed that hill with such exuberance that I thought he was trying to make me feel crazy.

I don't know how I managed to make it up that hill on such a sweltering afternoon. And I don't understand how that little old man could have. But somehow, both of us reached the top.

When I arrived, I expected to be through with surprises for the day. But I was wrong. First off, Ed just disappeared without a word of farewell. He had left my bag outside the bar that stood alone at the top of the hill. Its pink neon sign was blinking "Olivia's" across the front window—in the middle of a sunny afternoon!

Secondly, I was probably suffering heat stroke. Because I would not otherwise have entered a strange bar in a white town all alone. But when I stepped into Olivia's, all my senses took hold of me. The bracing aroma of garlic and onions worked like smelling salts, reviving me. I heard Patti Page singing one of my favorite songs through the stereo speakers. Glimmering wineglasses dangled from ceiling mounts like Christmas ornaments, reflecting the pink neon window sign that pulsed the bar's interior. Shiny blue, red, and amber liquor bottles lined a dozen mirrored shelves. A green-pelted pool table centered the room. And a soft breeze soothed my aching skin. I walked to the beautiful redwood counter and sat down.

My mind was sluggish from the meltdown day, so my thoughts were slow to form. All I remember thinking when I first looked around the bar was how extremely white everyone looked. It seemed that every patron glowed with whiteness, like self-illuminating porcelain. And it also seemed that most of them were trying very hard to appear as though they weren't noticing me. Finally, a broad-shouldered woman with long blonde hair and sad eyes approached me from behind the counter. She spread a flowery cocktail napkin before me and maintained a friendly demeanor, even after I mistakenly addressed her as "Miss Olivia."

"No, I'm not the owner," she said. "My name is Norma. Norma Halpern."

"I'm sorry, Norma," I said. "I just assumed . . ."

She nodded and graciously offered, "Don't worry. That's an all right enough mistake to make. Now, what can I get you?"

I smiled weakly and ordered a chicken salad sandwich. And I swallowed a tumbler of iced tea so fast that I choked on a lemon wedge—my body had become such a dry sponge. But Norma was attentive, and she poured me a second glass that I drank more leisurely. Minutes later, she returned with a towering sandwich. I hungrily bit into its moist chicken, piled high between thick slices of fresh sourdough.

While my body rehydrated and cooled toward life-compatible temperatures, Ella Strather came over and introduced herself. She sat beside me and began talking about Little Richard and Chuck Berry and Martin Luther King. Also, some recently recruited black guard with the Detroit Pistons. She told me that she loved soul food and the dynamism of urban living. "Hey, Norma," she called out, "put on that Nat King Cole record."

She was flat-out shocked when I matter-of-factly informed her that I was born in Deer Creek, Idaho. That I'd never been to New York or L.A. That I preferred classical music and cared nothing about basketball. A deafening silence followed—one that would prove to forever mark a vast and unbridgeable distance between us.

Ella anxiously double-backed then and seemed suddenly unsure about what to say. Then she rambled on nervously about all sorts of things. About Woodhaven's "fabled" history. Its winning high school football team. Its unwavering civic pride. She talked about the town's claim as the birthplace of Thalburg Gelatin.

At some point, I had to interrupt her and indicate my need to retire for the night. I politely tried to convey appreciation for her friendly intentions (although they had truly worn me out). After finally escaping her company, I ascended the stairs to my room, internally chanting, *That's an all right enough mistake.*

After settling into my room, I phoned Leonard and told him about everything that had happened that day. After reassuring him that I felt safe, I phoned the manager of the Yuba City Water Company to postpone my utility inspection. I switched on a rickety metal-bladed fan, and, after showering, collapsed onto fresh cotton sheets that were pulled taut across a large brass bed.

When I awoke at dawn, I heard the faint rumble of the skinny creek that ran through the town, aspiring to be the Baptista River. I fixed my hair, scrubbed and cocoa-buttered my face, and put on my cotton dress that I'd spot-washed and hung over the shower rod to dry. I descended the stairs and exited through the bar's unlocked front door.

Through the canyon's dense fog, I walked down the hill. I traced my route along the Baptista, back to the footbridge and the Polish bakery I had seen the day before. I bought freshly brewed coffee and two warm apricot pastries that were wrapped in wax paper twisted at the ends. I carried my treats to a park behind the bakery and sat on a bench near a statue commemorating local victims of the Holocaust.

And . . . well . . . it was the first time in years that I'd been by myself. Away from my job, and miles from my home in San Francisco, from my Leonard, from all things defining me. I felt like a paper doll that had been cut out from the scenery of her prior life and carried by strong winds to this peculiar new landscape.

And I was taken by such surprise . . . Soon, I began to experience sweet overwhelming relief in being freed from everything that had shaped my life before. Sitting on a strange park bench in a strange town full of strange white people who didn't know what to make of me, I felt unburdened of anyone's expectations—including Leonard's and my own. Being an unknown quantity in the world made me feel calm and peaceful.

But while feasting on this epiphany, out of nowhere, Ed Utley reappeared. How that odd little elf of a man located me and snuck up so soundlessly behind me *again*—well, it was, literally, a jolting mystery. He just handed over his bill, pointed to my Chrysler and said, "You can mail me a check if you don't have the money on you."

Frankly, I was disappointed that he had fixed my car sooner than predicted. But I thanked him profusely and promised to mail the check the moment I returned to San Francisco. I gathered what remained of my pastry, got into my car, and I drove slowly away. And although I steadily watched Ed through my rearview mirror, I swear, he instantly disappeared. Poof!

Months after that, my Leonard died. He left the
world in the flash of an aortic rupture. And, as I've
explained, I struggled to go on without him and believe in a survivable future. But the first time that I
performed a water inspection after *finally* returning to
work, I discovered I could not sign my name to au-
thenticate my report. I froze when I was supposed to
write "Mrs. Leonard Williams" on the signature line.
My hand refused to move the pen across the page.

That experience forced me to realize how desperately I needed to be convinced of who I was, independent of who I'd been with Leonard. I needed my life to
rub up against other people's lives in order to redefine
myself. And when I thought about where I could di-
vest my confused and tattered identity in hopes of
finding a new one, Ed Utley's visage appeared to me,
affecting me strangely.

The next morning, I telephoned my boss and quit
my job, applying my banked vacation days to cover
the requisite thirty days' notice. I gave my landlord
notice, too. In the afternoon, I drove to the used car
lot and exchanged the Chrysler for a red Mustang.

A week or so later, I drove to Olivia's Bar. And
this time, I addressed Norma correctly. She remembered me, too. We came to talking easily, and I was
surprised to hear that she had acquired ownership of
the bar the very day before. Still, a certain sobriety in
her voice made me hesitate to ask about the circumstances. She even changed the subject, asking me
about my old Chrysler. We laughed when I said that I
had just recently traded it in.

I was in no mood to explain my sorry situation.
So, I asked her straightaway if she knew about a

place I could rent for an indefinite period. She fell silent, and she looked at me with such intensely sympathetic curiosity that I just blurted out about Leonard dying. She handed me some tissues and placed her hands over mine, and then she told me how sorry she was. For a moment, she closed her eyes as if she were looking inside herself, and I felt that, at the same time, she was seeing me as well. I calmed down, and she tried to reassure me that, soon, I'd soon be "all right enough." Then she excused herself to use the phone by the grill. I watched her dial a number and heard her speak to someone in a somber, hushed manner. When she returned, she told me about a house for rent a block north of the park, near the Polish bakery.

I thanked her profusely. And within the hour, I was standing in front of that house. It was a cottage, really. A cottage of white stucco, surrounded by gardens and stippled with purple morning glories vines. I knocked timidly on the door because Norma said that the owner was feeling poorly but in a great hurry to leave. I didn't want to intrude.

I was surprised when the door opened to reveal a swollen-faced woman with long red hair who stood tall in the entry. She stared blankly at me, but her eyes seemed to convey a sadness even greater than my own. When I told her that Norma had sent me, she invited me in. She apologized for the mess in the house, explaining that she was planning on leaving Woodhaven within two days. And when she told me to call her "Olivia," I realized that she had been the owner of the bar.

She led me to the living room where her suitcases were spread open on the floor. I was so thoroughly stuck in my own sorrow that I had trouble summoning enough social grace to respond to hers. In fact, when I finally attempted to convey my sympathy, all I managed to do was blurt out that my Leonard had died.

"I'm sorry," Olivia replied, in a slow southern drawl that seemed to stop time itself. She placed a comforting hand on my arm, and we stood silently together while she scanned the living room, seeming to analyze its walls and ceilings with intense concentration. When we were somehow ready, she invited me to tour the rest of her cottage. And though we spoke very little, all the while we seemed to be communicating through mutual grief.

Just before we were about to exit the kitchen to explore the backyard gardens, she stopped and faced me directly. She took in a long deep breath and slowly exhaled. Then she offered me her cottage—all its furniture, its rugs and curtains, even the food in her pantry—for an unbelievably small settlement. I protested the sum—it was outrageously insufficient for such wonderful property and furnishings. I didn't want any part in taking advantage of her vulnerable state.

But she heard nothing of my objections. She insisted that it was "invaluable" for her to be free to leave town with all her business settled. Besides, she added, she took some comfort in knowing that it would be me living in her home. She said that Norma could handle any paperwork for us, and then she offered me the guest bedroom for the next two nights if I had nowhere else to stay.

On the spot, I withdrew my checkbook and wrote for the full amount. I handed my check to Olivia, feeling concerned about her welfare but too shy to inquire about her private business. In retrospect, that was an overly cautious mistake on my part. But, at the time, it seemed that my words and concerns were mostly obstacles in her path.

Olivia and I barely spoke over the ensuing two days. She spent most of her time sitting at the roll-top desk in her room, rewriting a note that she repeatedly tore up and threw away. On her last night there, I overheard her sobbing while on the phone, begging someone to, "Please, don't tell him." Several times, she haltingly managed, "We've done nothing wrong!" She kept apologizing for "ruining everyone's lives" and for what, she now knew, she had to do in order "to make things right."

The next morning, Olivia was gone.

I went to her kitchen and brewed coffee that I poured into a souvenir mug from Atlanta. I gathered Oat Flakes and canned milk from her pantry, eating them on the back porch while staring at her gardens. Later that afternoon, I rummaged through her closets and tried on her skirts and blouses and shoes. In the days that followed, I began to sift through the novels and poetry books that overfilled her cottage. By the end of the first week, I was weeding her gardens, picking her beefsteak tomatoes, and cooking her family recipes in her black-crusted pots. I found her trowel and clippers, and I began tending her squash and strawberries, sweet peas and herbs. For hours at a time, I listened to her records on her phonograph.

Months passed with me living within the shelter of Olivia's habits like this.

But one winter's morning, I awoke to the sound of heavy rain through the bedroom window. And, for the first time since living in Olivia's cottage, I heard the Baptista River flowing.

I threw on a robe and went outside, not caring about the rain, and only wanting to hear more of the river. Its bold rushing hum reawakened me to the day I first stumbled into Woodhaven, when Ed Utley guided me along the Baptista to Olivia's.

And while I stood on the porch, absorbing the rain and the river's hum, as surely as massive clouds moved overhead, something dark and heavy shifted inside me as well.

I went back into the house and started the coffee. Through the kitchen window, I noticed that Olivia's Japanese maple had turned to gold. I washed and dressed, ate a quick breakfast, and then I began re-arranging the furniture. I pushed Olivia's blue sofa next to the fireplace, and I draped my grandmother's shawl across it. I removed Olivia's iris curtains from the dining room and left the windows bare. I hung a photograph of Leonard on the wall above the mantel. And, to my surprise, at the end of that day, I said aloud to no one in particular, "This is my home." And I thanked Olivia for allowing me to rediscover my life by trying on hers.

The next day, I actually ventured into town. I shopped at Markowicz's Food Mart like a regular customer, using clipped coupons from the *Woodhaven Courier*. Later that week, I waited in a long line for bread loaves at Arlene's Good Baked Goods. And by year's end, I created a collage honoring African American history that was ceremoniously installed in the Thalburg Historical Museum.

During the subsequent years I spent here, I became Woodhaven's first African-American resident (at least, of official record). And two years ago—nearly five decades after I arrived—I championed a local political campaign to help elect our country's first black president! For years, I taught English and drama at Woodhaven High, and I was a regular judge for the annual Thalburg Gelatin recipe contests. I earned notoriety for my uniquely honed talent to sneak up on Ed Utley and scare *him* to death. And through no particular effort, I drove Ella Strather crazy all the while she wore me down with her perpetual need (and perpetual inability) to forge a close personal bond with me.

In the mid-'80s, I also enjoyed a pleasant (though brief) romance with Marcus Ellsworth, the high school chemistry teacher. That proved to be the only time I ever strayed from my Leonard. Marcus was a nice enough man, but the problem was . . . well, that he was a nice enough man. I always had to place his tentative hand on my knee whenever we sat together on the couch. And Marcus did not have Leonard's sweet stinky feet. He also had an unfortunate tendency to clear his throat before he spoke, as though he found it hard to get his words out. I tried to make things work well enough between us, and to enjoy what was there on its own merits. But my old desire for Leonard was irreplaceable at the level of my natural urges, and the pleasantries between Marcus and me ultimately dwindled.

Luckily, I had properly prepared for my financial independence. At the right time, I had invested wisely in zero-coupon bonds. I was even able to buy into the bakery when Annie needed a loan to add on an espresso bar. I promised her that I would be "the most silent partner" she could ever imagine—strictly hands-off management—and I only requested in return a nominal percent on the loan and permission to grab a pastry or coffee whenever I wanted.

Over the years, I have often thought about Olivia. I found myself praying that she had discovered relief from whatever tragedy had forced her to exile. And I'd fantasize about her returning one day to visit. I'd show her the changes I made to the cottage, and what had endured. I imagined her being pleased to see that I'd kept her morning glories lush on their trellises.

In the end, although I had moved to Woodhaven with hopes of disappearing, to my great surprise, I found myself immersed in a steady process of becoming. I kept discovering new parts of myself, and I became many different things to many different people. I kept sorting through what was mine and what was theirs—and, also, what was ours. And I saw how those categories frequently overlapped and shifted over time. I held a silent contract with the people who lived here, and the mistakes we all made with each other were mostly of the "all right enough" kind. My life moved on with their lives, and, often, because of them.

But now I must leave my cottage because of this awful flood. I must pick up and start all over again. My old friend of a river has turned against me.

I am grateful to have my sister waiting on me to join her in her retirement community in Berkeley. She's extended so many welcoming accommodations. She's even obtained permission from her co-op board for me to plant grafts from Olivia's vines in the central commons.

And I wish I could say that I feel good about that upcoming move—courageous and hopeful about whatever changes lie ahead. But I don't. I really don't.

As I look out at this torrential rain—at the downed branches from my Japanese maple, the vegetable gardens that have become a ghastly stew—I think about Leonard and Olivia, and I see my world being erased again.

And still, I will admit this much. That after decades of watching the Baptista move through its seasonal changes while I moved through mine, I've discovered that my life is carried forward by something greater than my own will and intention. I have discovered that I have thrived on surprise, and I keep relearning that I am more than my enduring love for Leonard.

⌐ romeo's kiss ⌐

NICHOLAS FENWAY ARCHER presses his long sad face against the Winnebago's rain-streaked rear window, despite his parents' stern directive to "stop looking back." He watches anxiously as the tar road mooring him to Woodhaven thins with each distancing mile that his parents drive toward their new home. It finally snaps when the trailer turns onto the interstate, severing his tie to the only world he has ever known. He falls back against hastily packed crates of kitchen utensils that are jammed into the Winnebago's rear cabin. A fizzy noise swirls inside his head, and his stomach churns. His blue eyes dim, abruptly emptied of their customary brightness. And the crack that for months has been ripping through his heart—the one that only Helen can mend—widens beyond measure.

In the trailer's front cabin, his parents' conversation grows louder by the minute. At intervals, its volume briskly expands, and their words billow toward him like toxic smoke, pressing him deeper into despair. In vain, he tries to ignore their peculiar dialect of rapidly interdigitating sentences. His mother begins, "I can't believe you took our egg poacher but left the Osterizer" and his father overlaps, "those milk crates we always use for step ladders!" They continue, ". . . then we finally change that light bulb in the hallway just before this"/ "flood happens—but who could've known"/ "to have time to really sort out what we should take"/ "the next exit."

Nick groans and wedges his body into a cramped space between the stereo cabinet and a box overfilled with gardening tools. But this shift in perspective only provides a better view of his parents' loathsome music collection—cartons of their vinyl LPs from the '60s and '70s that have *miraculously* failed to wear out in the Archer household.

He longs for his iPod now—as much for its sound-protective earbuds as for the healing antidote of his own music library. For days, electricity outages have also robbed him of saving online connections with his friends. Instead, he has had to bear uninterrupted contact with his incurably cheerful parents while they packed and boarded up their downriver home and sang their ancient songs *off-key*.

The prospect of spending *three more days* of tormenting intimacy with them inside the Winnebago is unbearable. He pulls his leather jacket over his head and presses it against his ears, but still his parents' irksome voices locate him like sonic stealth missiles: "At least we remembered Grandma's ashes"/ "that bowling trophy we won"/ "on our honeymoon in Sacramento"/ "such a great time back then, remember"/ "that friend of yours with the handle-bar mustache who—"

"Christ!" Nick yells. "Can you two stop? You're *torturing* me!"

His parents' conversation ends abruptly, and for several edgy moments he hears only pots and pans jangling, the Winnebago's yawning suspension, rain tapping the roof. Still, he cannot relax. He waits apprehensively for the expected next round of parental auditory assault.

His parents exchange bemused looks, as though surprised by an unexpected visitor. "Well, it seems our dear Nicky is here!" his mother says. His father calls out, "Hey, buddy—good to hear you're alive back there."

Nick barely cages his irritation, and he tries not to scream. But the taut veins around his skull begin to protest the task of keeping his mind intact. Finally, he turns toward his parents and explodes. "*Dear?* I begged you to never call me that!" The pressure mounting behind his eyes threatens to blind him with rage. "And, *Nicky?* You know that's off limits, too!"

Countless times before, he has pleaded with his parents to stop addressing him as "dear" or "honey" or "baby." Last year, during his sixteenth birthday celebration, he officially "went on record" with them—that he had outgrown their diminutive endearments and would no longer accommodate them. Being a man now, he deserved to be addressed as an adult. And that they, of all people—from a generation extolling individual freedom and *still* singing about rebellion—*they* should fully understand his need to feel free of their claims.

Besides, privately, he also felt that any right to speak those endearments to him belonged exclusively to someone else. To Helen—beautiful, sweet Helen whose lush lips could properly shape them in a manner befitting his mature desires.

"Can you pull over at the next gas station?" Nick asks.

His father begins: "Well, son, that's pretty bad timing"/ "yes, hon—oops, *Nick*—we just turned onto the interstate and there's no"/ "not another exit for several miles and"/ "funny, I don't remember your bladder being so small," his mother finishes.

"You're driving me insane!" he bemoans. "Please—just pull over."

In unison, his parents shrug their shoulders. Then his father winks at his mother and says, "Barbara, I think a teenage boy might get embarrassed when his mother mentions his *bladder*." And, as though entrusted with a tribal male secret, she places a finger across her lips and nods reverently.

Nick's eyes roll wildly, trying to escape the reality pressing against them. With dramatic abandon, he slumps over a crate labeled "fragile" and tells himself that the people sitting in the front seat must be aliens. It is the only sensible explanation. Yes—drunken Doctor McCracken must have switched him at birth and separated him from his true and *extremely normal* parents.

"Son," his father booms, trying to locate him in the rearview mirror. "How about you and me just pulling to the side of the road and writing our names together in this flood?"

Nick feels like a lab animal, trapped inside an evil scientist's experiment to test the limits of sanity. He feebly manages, "All I want is a bathroom. Just an honest-to-god actual bathroom."

"Honey," his mother begins, "can't you wait until we"/ "make it to Glen Cove?" his father concludes.

Raising his head above the family's jumbled belongings to look at his parents, he resists an urge to respond in a way he would surely regret later. His words strain through clenched teeth: "I'm dead serious. With my hand on my future grave. Please get me to a freakin' bathroom."

He sees his parents nod and, seconds later, the Winnebago reverses direction. Although their inimitable dialogue resumes, it becomes hushed and indistinct. Soon, the trailer pulls into a gas station, its engine quiets, and he hears his father instruct the attendant, "Might as well fill her up, buddy."

Nick bolts out through the rear of the Winnebago. He runs into the men's room and locks the door. Clutching the dingy porcelain sink, he tries to steady his reeling mind. But he knows he won't survive the car trip, let alone the strange new future into which he is being transported.

He checks his watch, aware that his parents will not wait long in the trailer. They have allotted only three days to haul their collective lives to Uncle Jim's farm in Nebraska. He has visited his uncle's place several times before, for Archer family annual reunions that progressively diminished in size. But the severe flatness of his uncle's land always disturbed him. Once, he even dreamt that it suddenly decompressed, erupting into three proper dimensions and propelling him into space. It was untenable to imagine living on such a treacherously horizontal surface—one that would only become impossibly flatter without Helen there beside him.

Staring into the clouded mirror above the sink, he agonizes, *Why is love so painful?* He presses a hand over his chest, but his desire continues to pour out from his wounded heart, filling him completely, and, in a breathtaking flash, it floods him. Then a bold resuscitating knock on the door thoroughly rattles him. He is forcibly returned to his familyland drama when he hears, "Son—you still in the john?"

Forced to imagine his father on the other side of the door, he experiences Helen's swift exile from his thoughts. It was just impossible to hold these two people within the same mindscape. And it was Helen's vital presence that he required now.

He paces the floor, trying to collect himself, trying to fend off his identity as the de-facto son of the obtuse man knocking on the door. Finally, he snaps. "No, I'm in Disneyland! I'm in . . . in Paris! On Jupiter. I'm—"

"Whoa, son!" his father says, shifting into his sincere, benevolent, fatherly voice. "I know it's all upsetting—everything. Your mother and I understand how hard this move is on you. Listen, you just take your time in there."

"Go away," Nick pleads.

"All right, Nicholas," his father says. "You know we love you, son—your mother and me."

Could he possibly say that any louder? Did EVE-RYONE get a chance to hear him? Why not broadcast my last name, too? Tell the whole world that I'm stuck like a freakin' idiot in some gas station bathroom . . .

With relief, he finally hears his father's work boots strike a retreat. And after the footsteps fade, Helen reclaims the space of his thoughts and feelings—hers uniquely to stake. *Helen.* Tall, strong, curvaceous Helen whose golden hair flows down her back like a silken waterfall. Soft-lipped, full-lipped, crimson-lipped Helen whom he once *almost* kissed. Helen, whose delicious moan—as he's often imagined it—he *surely* would have elicited had he not blown his lines during the play's opening night:

Then move not while my prayer's effect I take.

Thus from my lips by thine my sin is purged.

But he had forgotten his lines. When the occasion arose to speak them, his mind froze. Instead, with his parted lips poised inches away from Helen's, he stood paralyzed and mute like a stunned animal on the high school gymnasium's stage. He stared into Helen's increasingly quizzical eyes and watched a bemused but tender expression spread across her face. He groped desperately for his lines that were supposed to guide his lips toward hers, igniting Helen's desire and sealing their love. But the words would not materialize. He felt inept and foolish in his crimson leotards, all the while cameras flashed throughout the auditorium and classmates jeered. All he could think about was his pathetic belittlement becoming immortalized in cyberspace, viral on YouTube.

The beguiled grin that fully broke across Helen's face only intensified his terror. "Hey, Romeo," she had whispered, trying to rouse him out of his predicament. "Come on, Nick. Kiss me."

Still, all he could summon was additional panic. And he feared that, even if he should somehow manage to kiss her, his long-throttled passion would erupt in an embarrassing 3-D public display. He didn't even hear the stage prompter cuing his lines. Finally, Sam, his understudy, appeared and tapped him on the shoulder. "Yo, Romeo," he whispered, "take a hike."

Nick hazily exited the stage to the sidelines where his drama teacher, Mrs. Williams, was waiting. But her sympathetic look was too much to engage. So he looked away, back toward the stage—regrettably, just in time to witness Sam kiss Helen and to hear Helen reply:

Then have my lips the sin that they have took.

It was too extreme to hear Helen speak "lips" and "sin" so close together. One word rubbed hotly against the other, stoking unwieldy urges inside him. He felt that he could become human fireworks. But then a wash of indignation extinguished the sparks when Sam kissed Helen a *second* time! Without thinking, he emerged from the sidelines protesting, "That's not in the script!"

An eerie hush prevailed inside the auditorium. Fellow actors and intrigued audience members focused their wide-eyed attention on Nick. *Oh God*, he despaired as he absorbed their collective scrutiny. Then

Mrs. Williams appeared and placed a steadying arm around him. She guided him back to the sidelines—but not before Sam flashed him a shrewd grin and kissed Helen *again* to the audience's delight.

NICK OPENS THE RESTROOM DOOR and peers cautiously out. Pewter clouds suspend from an indifferent sky, and raindrops quiver in the air. He ambles toward the gas pump that is furthest from his parents' waiting trailer, pretending not to notice when his mother's head pops through the window. To stall his return to the Winnebago, he takes a circuitous path around displays of windshield wipers and antifreeze, chanting internally with each dawdling step, *What am I going to do?*

Thwacking thunder rocks the sky. Looking up, he sees the exit sign for Berringer's Bridge across the road and a marker stone at its base. He crosses the street and clears the curious stone with sweeps of his boots, uncovering an embedded bronze plaque that reads:

"In loving memory
of my parents and aunt.
Go with God.
May 16, 1970"

He stares at the plaque, its glint alternately fading and re-appearing with reflected traffic light. And *Go with God* blazes in his heart. *Go with God* resounds in his head.

Looking to the long procession of cars fleeing Woodhaven along interstate 20, he thinks: *Go with God*. Scanning the watery tartop, the bent tree lines, the wonky telephone poles, he internally chants, *Go with God*.

But then a summoning honk from his parents' Winnebago claims his attention. He stares once more at the commemorative plaque before reluctantly returning to the trailer. And when he passes by the driver's window, his father winks and doffs his Red Sox cap.

"Please, dad—let's just go," Nick flatly responds.

His father nods his all-knowing nod. Then his mother begins, "Good, honey, because we really need"/ "some privacy sometime"/ "but we have to get on the road"/ "a man needs a moment here and there"/ "to get a move on"/ "before dark," his father finishes.

Nick shuffles to the rear of the Winnebago and opens its back door. He pushes aside a resettled crate. "Okay," he says, before slamming the door shut.

The trailer pulls away from the gas pump and reenters its trajectory toward Nebraska. From his position behind a motor oil display, Nick watches the Winnebago bounce over a pothole as it exits the station and chugs back toward interstate 20, a puff of exhaust trailing from its fuel pipe.

Go with God circulates through Nick while he runs the slippery road from the gas station, back toward Woodhaven and Thalburg Canyon. His sure steady breathing becomes a rasp-cut parting his way, and his body slices through the air. *Helen, with love's light wings . . .*

He leaps over newborn creeks that shimmy on watery legs. He scrambles over moss-covered river rocks. He sidesteps a jelly jar and flashlight, punts a coffee can brimming with Saran wrap, hurdles a barbed-wire fence and races through the Dunleavys' apple orchard.

Nearing the treacherous riverbank, his heel catches on a cornhusk sheaf, and he skis clumsily along the slick ground before plummeting headfirst into stone-strewn mud. He rights himself, wipes his face with fistfuls of brown leaves, and rubs spit across the new gash above his right knee. Bracing himself, he limps several paces until he reenters his prior cadence . . . *Go with God, Go with God* . . . He sprints behind Ed Utley's place . . . *For stony limits cannot hold love out* . . .

Finally in sight of Helen's home and spotting candlelight in its windows, he collapses. He leans against a tree stump, waiting for his heart to still, watching for Helen to appear in the window, saying to himself: *A thousand times the worse to want thy light.*

And yet, how worrisome to see the Baptista butting against Helen's front yard. When he last waited outside her home in hopes of catching a glimpse of her, he had stood on a dry rise of land a few feet away that is now completely obliterated by floodwater.

A metallic whine sounds, and Helen's front door opens. Two small circles of flashlight bounce through the doorway and wiggle on the porch. He hears Helen's laconic father say, "I'll be right back. No more than an hour." The two light beams separate—Helen's remaining on the porch, her father's tracking the driveway. A car door slams, an engine revs, and their rumbling sedan pulls away.

Nick panics when he sees Helen turn back toward the house. While feeling pathetically unprepared to speak to her, he is also unprepared to let her go. He wants to run to her, wrap his powerful arms around her and kiss her finally. He wants her to feel the press of his life and body against hers.

But, just like before, his unwieldy desire short-circuits his intentions. He stands paralyzed, brimming with impotent urges.

Even when Helen places a hand on the door—and despite how harshly he berates himself—still, he cannot move. He thinks he must be afflicted with constitutional timidity that merely worsens with desire. Or born with flawed circuitry between his heart and head and body. No wonder, then, that he has always overestimated his chances with Helen. No wonder that his relentless longing merely wears down his heart and spirit.

Give her up, he counsels himself. *I cannot live my life with such excruciating intensity forever.*

He looks to the ground, intending to limit further witness of Helen. And he waits—it seems forever—for the sound of her door closing to mark the moment of her departure from his life.

But silence prevails. Agonizing silence that intensifies during successive overlong moments. Finally, he looks curiously back to Helen's house—in time to witness something a thousand times worse than the suffering he had tried to avoid. He sees Helen on the porch, candlelight radiating a corona around her, and she stares up at the night sky, looking exquisitely solitary and peaceful.

He has stumbled unwittingly upon proof—brutal, appalling, unwelcome proof—that she is complete without him. Seeing her in such blissful solitude violently confirms his irrelevance to her happiness. He thinks his pain cannot get worse, but it does when she begins to sing:

You are my lucky star.

I saw you from afar . . .

It's killing him to see her so full of joy when his presence is not required. Her singing pierces his heart, and he hears it above whips of wind and the growling river. He drops to his knees, stifling his agony, waiting for her to stop. Then abruptly, the front door slams and Helen disappears into the house.

Thunder bellows ominously, lightning illuminates the canyon in staggered images, and suddenly he is worried about his physical safety. After gazing at Helen's home a final time, he heads back along the river toward his family's boarded-up home, resolving to spend the night there. In the morning, he will hike to the Red Cross shelter at the high school, tell the Sheriff about his circumstances, and await his parents' punishing return.

He follows a canyon path that he has walked a million times before. He fantasizes about dry socks, a warm flannel shirt, the floppy old sofa they left behind in the family den, and whatever cereal boxes remain in the pantry. He leaps over the Dunleavys' fence and crosses their bloated strawberry fields, pulling his T-shirt up over his nose to staunch the smell of rotting vegetation.

When he nears Maddy's cabin, he hears a radio playing. He studies the cabin's curiously unlit windows and, concerned that she may still be inside, he ascends the hill, calling out her name. He knocks on the front door which displays a bold note: "Nobody home! Go away!" Receiving no response, he walks along the cabin's perimeter, but sees only residual evidence of yet another neighbor's life upturned by the flood.

He turns away and shuffles back down the hill. Moments later, he is chanting again, *Go with God*. The chant fuels his spirit, accelerates his steps, and he breaks into a sprint when he reenters the canyon path. *Go with God* carries him, he becomes lightfooted. And without conscious intent, he abruptly turns around and runs back toward Helen's home.

Holding the image of Helen singing to the starry sky, he moves faithfully and steadily toward her. *It is my soul that calls upon thy name* now resounds in his head. He maneuvers around a red motorboat that is moored to a jetty. He vaults over a wall of sandbags surrounding Helen's house. *It is my soul that calls upon thy name*, his mind whispers. He hurdles the front fence, slogs across swampy lawn, sidesteps jumbled woodpiles and bounds toward Helen's porch, moving confidently in the direction of his longing.

But a dense thudding darkness descends on him, and he flinches. A moment passes before he identifies it as the shadow that Helen casts through the front window. The darkness drapes across his chest, brushes his lips, rolls across his legs. He opens his arms to embrace it and whispers, "So thrive my soul!" He consumes her shadow, he inhales it. His skin absorbs it, and it rushes throughout his body to all un-touched places. He feels it inside his heart as it be-gins to mend the crack that has been tearing through it. Newly emboldened, he starts again toward her porch, chanting, *But that a joy . . . Past joy . . . Calls out to me!*

But when his boot lands with the full weight of his zeal on the lowermost step, a strange explosion sounds. He hears spine-chilling primitive cries, gelat-inous inhuman sounds and squawks. He looks toward the source of the cacophony, discovering dozens of caged and wild-eyed chickens in the back of a flatbed truck. His glands dump all their adrenaline at once as the front door also flings open and Helen emerges. She shoots a rifle toward the sky, and, before he can speak, she shoots again. Reflexively, he turns away and flees. He leaps back over the woodpiles, pulling his jacket over his head to evade her witness of his idiocy. Trying to outrun her flashlight, he vaults over the fence and sandbag wall. And just when he thinks that he might have escaped her detection, he hears her call out, "Nick? Nicky Archer? Is that you?"

He runs faster and farther, cursing himself all the while that Helen's words trail behind: "Come back! I won't shoot!" He runs until all he hears is his heart thumping against his eardrums, his breath scraping his windpipes. Finally, he falls exhausted to the ground and shouts, "I'm so fucked!"

He looks plaintively to the evening sky, now so dark that it almost merges with the inky river. Shame refills him and he bellows repeatedly, "I am so fucked!"

Brisk winds whoosh through the canyon. He is so far away from where—and with whom—he had hoped to be tonight. He wishes he could simply re-enter his old life, like Jimmy Stewart in the Christmas movie his parents always watch. He wants to fall asleep in his old bunk bed. Play his saxophone. Even see his obtuse and maddening parents again.

He knows that, whatever happens now, he must rid his heart of Helen if he is to survive the future without her. In a symbolic gesture, he stands, places a hand across his chest, and yanks her out of his heart. Then he pitches his hand toward the river and releases her. But his arm overswings and his body follows its powerful arc. Helplessly, he teeters forward, unable to secure footing on the slippery riverbank. Wind thrashes the tall grasses as he tumbles headfirst into the Baptista.

The river's commanding currents seize him, and he struggles to keep his head above water. The night chill scorches his skin, a watery film covers his eyes, his forehead smacks against a footbridge, and, in a flash, he is carried downstream. The Baptista violently drags him down. He opens his eyes, he closes his eyes, but the darkness is the same.

In the moment he expects to be his last, he envisions Helen, and that summons inside him a final desire that renews his strength. He pulls himself to the river's surface, coughing out water. Moonlight flutters in phantasmal shapes within his bleary view. He throws his arms into the air, thinking *Helen*.

Something grazes his hand. A moonlight ghost— something white and shimmering that touches his hand. He reflexively grabs it and does not let go. It yanks him up and out of the Baptista, and a moment later it drops him back into the river. Automatically, he stacks one hand above the other to pull himself up along the pale ghost. Finally, he seizes the tree limb from which the ghost suspends, and he hoists himself onto it. Crackled bark pierces his hands and cheek as he shimmies up along the limb. But he feels no particular pain because everything hurts at once and blurs all anatomic distinctions.

A sibilant sound circulates inside his head while he scuttles to the crook at the limb's base. Finally, leaning against the giant cedar's trunk, he struggles to catch his breath as he also struggles to determine whether he is dreaming, delirious, or perhaps even dead.

His past parades by—in dream or in thought, he cannot tell. His brass saxophone in its black velvet case. His cigar box filled with river stones. His track and field trophies. His favorite blue denim shirt patched at the elbows. His private sanctuary in the West Ridge hills . . .

Now he vaguely registers that he is perched like a bird in a towering tree. A delusion or an illusion? He's never understood the difference, but he knows that both are unhealthy to entertain. He gropes the limb on which he straddles, finding something made of cloth. He draws it toward him, remembering now the ghost that yanked him from the river. Memories of the day rush by—his parents' Winnebago lurching away, a bronze plaque on a roadside marker, slippery cornhusks, gunshots, crazed squawking chickens, woodpiles and sandbags, Helen . . .

Still, he must be dreaming or hallucinating. Because he is, after all, up in a tree, holding a wedding gown, surrounded by rising floodwater below. No other explanations could suffice. He closes his eyes and wonders where he is, *if* he really is, and how long a person could survive in a tree. *Helen*, he dreams or he thinks. Now envisioning himself drawing her close, he hears her whisper *Nick*. They are about to kiss and she says, *Nick Archer? Is that you?*

But, no . . . that's not what she'd say. Still, it occurs to him now that those *were* the words he last heard her speak while he was alive. He hears himself think or perhaps answer aloud, *Helen, that wasn't me.* He hears her summoning voice, *Nick, come back*, while imagining her looking into his eyes. Like an incantation, she repeatedly calls out his name, and each time he joyfully answers, *Yes!* He visualizes them embracing and professing their mutual love, and he hears or imagines that he hears her answer— *Hey, Nick! You goofball!*

Such obnoxious unscripted lines keep intruding! He rewinds the story in his head, and again his desiring lips wait on hers. She whispers . . . *Knucklehead!*

Stop interfering! he admonishes the undisciplined forces that meddle with his mindset. *What she says is, 'I love you, Nick.' And then she calls me 'dear.'* Now he leans into her, and she says, so softly, *Hey, dude— you with the dress.*

Outraged by yet another rude misspeak, he bolts upright and opens his eyes. But they are flooded with light in a manner suggesting imminent death in the movies. He says, "Oh, no," and instantly regrets making such a lame remark on the brink of his oblivion.

But then the light recedes and shines on Helen. She is sitting inside a red motorboat, looking up at him.

He studies her for a long moment, trying to figure out whether she exists outside of his mind.

"Nick?" she shouts above the motor's thrum. "It's me—Helen Cantor!"

He contemplates the wedding gown in his hands and the tree that he inhabits. And he concludes that Helen is a product of his fevered invention.

"Are you all right?" she yells. "What are you doing up there?" When she turns her flashlight back on him, he startles and lets go of the wedding gown. It drops and suspends from the tree limb again.

"Climb down that," Helen says. "Hurry up."

Her urgency pierces his befuddlement. And, like a Rubik cube, his brain snaps into right order. Now he knows he is not dreaming his odd reality. He weakly calls down, "Helen—it's you."

A familiar bemused expression breaks across her face. "Come on," she coaxes, extending her arms toward him.

Resigning himself to his awkward predicament, he scales down the wedding gown ghost. He falls into Helen's arms but sets the boat off-balance, nearly tipping them over.

"Whoa!" she says, steadying him and the boat. Then she wraps a blanket around him and says, "Thank God I found you."

He stares wordlessly back and thinks, *This boat will sink with the weight of my idiocy*. While unsure about what to say or do, he is surprised to remember now the lines he had failed to say to her before:

Then move not while my prayer's effect I take.

Thus from my lips by thine my sin is purged.

But those words feel strangely synthetic now, distant from his actual feelings. He scrambles for something to say that won't sound too inept, but all he manages is, "Thank you."

She smiles and says, "It might be better if you rest and not try to talk right now."

Although he nods agreement, he urgently desires to talk with her, using words that are authentically his. And while he struggles to locate them, she precipitously leans toward him, her silken hair brushing his face. He closes his eyes, inhales deeply, and readies his lips that have been waiting so long for hers.

But then she kisses him on the nose. It happens so quickly, that when he opens his eyes, she has already pulled away. With the steam of her breath still lingering between them, she revs up the motorboat, repositions the rudder and says, "Ready?"

The small red boat turns back against the strapping currents, and Nick and Helen focus their attention upstream.

Nick leans into the Baptista's husky spray, his ears filling with the riot of river and wind. He stares straight ahead. Everything is beginning to look so reassuringly uncertain.

submerged text

THE JOSHIPURAS SIT atop their antique Mission dining table, dangling their legs off one side, irritably kicking the floodwater.

Chandra scolds, "Flood insurance! Guaranteed replacement cost coverage! That is precisely what I instructed you to buy!"

Raj hangs his head. He knows she is right. Still, how many times must he endure her rebuke and admit his mistake? What additional penance must she extract from him?

Still, she repeats her complaint, and it lands like a missile on his last nerve. He explodes, "Enough! You are reminding me every minute of my error. I concede your great wisdom and my great foolishness." He slams a foot in the floodwater for emphasis.

She only yells back. "Damn it, Raj! We have lost everything! We have nothing now."

He silently counts to ten and says, "Chandra—*my dear, dear wife*—we both agree that I made a mistake. A *huge* mistake! Perhaps the worst mistake the world has ever known. I *admit* it. I forgot to buy the insurance coverage you asked for, and I did not—"

"But you told me you had taken care of it!" she fumes. "You lied to me, Raj!"

An Arctic silence encases them. Raj looks at his wife, registers her frozen grimace, and is reminded of his parents warning him as a child that prolonged pouting could settle permanently on one's face. He knows it is ill-timed to share this memory with Chandra now. It is better to stay on the track of her anger's predictable course and rely on the usual dynamics that have sustained them through arguments before.

"I'm sorry, Chandra. But really, how many times must I say it? Tell me what number you have in mind. I honestly thought I'd get around to it. I've just been so busy—"

"'Busy'?" she scoffs. "You had time to fill up countless boxes with your writings and screenplays and silly poems—"

"No, they are limericks," he corrects her.

She slaps his shoulder and continues, "Yes—your *Indian* limericks! What nonsense. No one cares about such things. The only purpose they ever served was to give publishers a good laugh at you. And then your ridiculous letters to editors to all those newspapers all over the country—"

"Hey," he protests, "some of them were published!"

"You have two, three—who knows, a dozen? —unfinished novels. And still—*still* you didn't have time to write one small application to our insurance company?"

Raj falls silent listening to his wife's strident inventory of his beloved writing projects now forever lost to the flood. "Washed out as a writer" comes to mind as he considers his current circumstances. He scans the cardboard boxes on the floor that contain his life's work—all sunken treasures suddenly. All the pretty words, the eureka words, the long-thought-out and sought-out words that he so painstakingly marshaled into precise sentences that filed neatly across yellow legal pads—they run together chaotically, forming undecipherable compositions. Beautiful wild phrases he had captured in cursive blue ink look like craggy veins bleeding across the pages. His warped manuscripts huddle together like spent, bloated storytellers. His archive of opinion columns for the *Woodhaven Courier* forms a subdued, soggy hillscape against the hallway baseboards. Index cards on which he catalogued inspirational quotes from favorite authors offer only cryptic guidance. And, with sad finality, he acknowledges that his five unfinished novels have become officially, permanently, "unfinished."

"If you don't understand about my writing," he says, "then you—"

"Yes, yes, yes. 'Then you don't understand *me*'," she finishes.

He grits his teeth and continues. "You have never appreciated my—"

"Your *precious* writing," she interrupts.

"Stop mocking me!"

But she persists. "What—five words? twenty? — maybe just marking a few checkboxes on an insurance application? I am incredulous! Ten minutes tops of your *precious* writing time."

He braces himself against further provocation. Looking to the living room, he seeks a diversion from powerful urges that coax him toward fury. He studies the tobacco-colored floodwater licking their coffee table. The wallpaper that bubbles and sags like bad skin. Everything smells like rotting fish and fusty newspaper. Loose pages from his notebooks drift languidly by.

But he is reeled back into his wife's despair when she laments, "We'll *never* recover from this! And it is your fault entirely."

He meets her stormy expression that, he fears, will set permanently in his memory. Hoping to prevent that, he purposively re-envisions her in a more appealing manner, recalling how beautiful she looked when they first met on the Sutlej River bank. How her tender brown eyes reflected glints of summer sun. How happy she looked when he promised her weeks later, "I will take you to America as my bride. To a place as green as the Vindhya valley. To a river as alive as the Sutlej."

At the time, his promise was audacious. But for an outdated map of California that he had removed from a *National Geographic*, he possessed no claim to

America. Even more problematic was the fact of their arranged marriages to other villagers, and the likelihood of being disowned by their parents if they did not comply.

Dutifully, Raj reenters the strained discussion with Chandra—though bearing an ultimatum that risks her greater fury. He says, "I will give you five more minutes. Five uninterrupted minutes to criticize me for not obtaining flood insurance and guaranteed whatever. But that is my limit. Say whatever you want, but say it in 300 seconds—less, preferably. Go ahead. Begin." He stares defiantly at her.

The crisp tick of the cabinet clock is all that sounds for several seconds. Then Chandra lets loose: "I can't believe you put us in harm's way! I trusted you! The few family heirlooms we had—*gone!* And all the hand-made furniture we commissioned? Our beloved books and music. Our *shoes*, Raj! You are my husband, and you are supposed to protect us. Look over there— my favorite evening bag drifting by the stove! Our photo albums are destroyed. Our food is floating in the kitchen . . ."

While she persists in itemizing their losses, his suffering expands exponentially. The mounting financial toll she computes already exceeds a sum beyond which any additional material loss is meaningless. Worse, she sounds like a robotic newscaster, hysterically conveying bad economic news. And she misses the point—using cold mathematical renderings that do not reflect the great personal cost of his private losses.

Indeed, he thinks—and, as Chandra claims—they have lost "everything." But they possess different notions of what "everything" means. He is troubled—no, deeply hurt—by her persistent omission of his writing as a lost item of value. It does not even merit her mention, all the while she catalogues the loss of five-dollar lampshades or dollar-store garden hats.

Finally, he can no longer tolerate it. He forcefully interrupts, "No insurance money could ever compensate me for the loss of my writing."

Chandra stifles an urge to blurt out unkindly: *Because insurance companies only insure valuables!* Still, she cannot pretend to share his loss—not after he has dismissed the importance of protecting their entire home. It is impossible to feel empathic when his suffering privileges what he has created in his sheltered solitude, during countless hours of insistent separation from her. She rues the fact that she has had to live so much of their marriage on a parallel stage because of his rigid need to write. And it was *she* who was left to wash *their* dishes. *She* who cleaned *their* house. It was *she* who answered *their* phone, cooked *their* meals, managed *their* social engagements, tended *their* gardens—all the while he wrote in his precious carved-out isolation. Her friend Ella was right after all—she should have more forcefully demanded Raj's attention and make it known how lonely she felt.

She sees Raj staring at her now as though from a distance. And she wonders if he is trying to control her with his aggressive silence, trying to manipulate her like a character in one of his novels. But yielding now with a show of sympathy would only be that—a show. And if truth be told, she must admit—she has long fantasized about a catastrophe like the current one to purge their home of his enormous clutter of manuscripts. She has imaginatively welcomed natural disasters that would select his writing for ruin. A wildfire targeting only his papers. A tornado blowing them out through the windows and into outer space. An earthquake cracking open the floor beneath his filing cabinets. Many times, she even daydreamed about hiring thieves to steal away his crates of notebooks, newspaper clippings, and Indian "limericks." And now, surveying the destructive handiwork of this actual flood, she feels somewhat vindicated. She thinks, *This unbidden act of God attests to the righteousness of my feelings.*

With as much self-censoring as she can muster, she says, "Yes, you are correct, Raj. But insurance coverage—*if* we had it—could help us replace a few practical items so we could, say, *live like human beings!* Things like food and dishes and soap. A sofa. Chairs. *Our beds—*"

"Enough!" Raj barks with finality. "You either accept my apology and we move on, or . . ."

"Or *what*?" she challenges.

But he has no good answer and becomes uncharacteristically speechless. He is surprised to find that he does not even care to complete his own sentence. Disquieting doubt shakes his great faith in words.

Chandra looks unflinchingly back, stunned to find him—*finally*—at a loss for words. *Perhaps that will make him sympathize with me for once.*

He looks away from the dark stones of her eyes and tries to shore himself up by resurrecting something, anything, that he wrote. But it is all submerged now, along with his once-saving identity as a writer. Still, he tries to resuscitate characters he once wrote into existence, hoping to be reminded of the power of his words to give life and meaning to theirs. He yearns to feel what his writing created for them—love, tranquility, happiness, courage—something other than this numbing despair, this aching nothingness. But, in the end, all he lamely says to Chandra is, "Or . . . I suppose we spend the rest of our lives sitting on this table, repeating the same sad things, over and over."

Chandra painfully recalls the lonely years she has spent accommodating his solitude. She glances at the mahogany cabinet encasing the clock on which Tomasz Podroski engraved his wish for them—to "always have time together." She snaps, "So now, *after* we have lost everything . . . *now* you might have time to spend with me, sitting on this table—"

"Okay!" he shouts. "If that is what you want, let's have at it. I'll start. *'I'm sorry.'* Now it's your turn, Chandra. Repeat your—"

She rolls her eyes and turns away, continuing her register of loss. Mostly, she thinks about the mementos she kept from the few vacations he had been willing to take away from his writing. The serving plates they bought from a stooped Sicilian potter. Hand-woven baskets from roadside stands in Taos. The cobalt blue vase they lugged home from New York. The *Bhagavad Gita* they recovered from her parents' home in Delhi.

"Come on!" he persists. "You are supposed to say, 'You should have bought flood insurance and replacement cost coverage!'"

"Stop," she says.

"No. You know your line: 'You should have bought'—"

"Your apology does not satisfy me."

"*Satisfy*?" he scoffs. "You actually think we are anywhere near the luxury of 'satisfying' one another? Frankly, I am worried about basic survival together."

A familiar tipping point is reached, and Chandra feels pushed over the edge by a critical mass of overwhelming futility in trying to communicate with Raj. Then her heart sinks precipitously, dragging with it her capacity to think. Finally, tears form and they trail down her face—the customary signal of her submission to the reign of her emotions.

Raj recognizes that customary signal and what must happen next. He knows they are retreating now into their separate lives, lived on separate tectonic plates. He watches a tear enlarge under Chandra's chin, and it seems to hang there forever like a tenacious bead of glue. Its maddening refusal to drop off provides irritating testimony of her consummate ability to *feel* everything. But this time—*this time*—he vows he will not allow her precious feelings to trump the rational discussion they must have in order to resolve the impasse between them. And he will not permit her emotional excesses to cancel out the deliberation required to bail themselves out of their dire circumstances. He has had it with her ubiquitous emotions, her indiscriminate tearfulness. Throughout their two decades of marriage, he has longed for her passionate companionship in language. He has yearned for affecting verbal exchanges that pass intimately and provocatively between them. But even in the most romantic of moments, when a select word or two rightly whispered in his ear might have given him great delight, she had only "felt" her desire for him.

Chandra despises the wordless space in which she lands whenever she free-falls down through the tunnel of her emotions. She is desperate to grab onto words to break her descent and stay in contact with her husband. But she always falls too fast, losing out to the strong gravitational pull of feeling.

Raj stares blankly at stacks of his buried texts that appear spectral under the floodwater. He hopes that Chandra will not drop into her abyss of feeling because, frankly, he has neither the will nor strength to rescue either of them with his usual armory of words. He needs her to come to him now, bearing language and saving words of her own. Yet, he hears nothing but her dispiriting silence. And all he sees is the usual clouded look in her eyes whenever she turns inward and escapes to the solitary place she inhabits during their quarrels.

With mounting resentment, he reflects on Chandra's devaluation of his writing. And how in the past she has always viewed it with suspicion or jealousy—never understanding it as *his* key to self-preservation. *For twenty years, I have worked hard to provide us a good life—cleaning and drilling teeth, talking for hours to patients who can't talk back. And for what understanding or gratitude from her?*

On countless occasions, writing has rescued him from the tedium and despair of his day job. Communicating with the characters he created—even if imagined—served as an antidote to his loneliness. He loved crafting their fascinating lives and complex experiences, and he lived them vicariously. He was happy to transport them to landscapes more exotic than the dental office he rented above the food mart. Through his writing, he explored issues more compelling than dental hygiene, events more riveting than eroding enamel, human behaviors more intriguing than flossing habits.

He hears his deep fatigue counseling him: *No words can save you now.* Drawing his legs to his chest and resting his head on his knees, he wonders if *this* is how his marriage ends. On *this* table. In *this* flood. Drowning in *this* deadly silence.

Chandra knows that he expects her to say something anything at all, really, because it never matters. It is always predestined to be the wrong thing to say. *All he ever wants is for me say a few flawed words that he can attack, just to avoid having to respond to my feelings.*

Still, his strange quietude begins transporting her to an unversed moment. And once there, she realizes that, for the first time, she is not girding herself against the usual rush of his punishing words. She feels the powerful tide of her emotions pulling back, even reversing its usual direction toward him. She can sense the wild sea of her feelings shore up, and she is not worried now about drowning in them.

Raj is suddenly aware of a remarkable connecting silence between them, one that not even he wishes to transform with words.

A new stillness floods them. And neither of them rushes in to vanquish the silence, or fill it with automatic grievances.

Then fierce light bursts through the living room window, and the sound of an approaching vehicle captures their attention. Through the storm-cracked pane, they track a white Winnebago passing by the house within an illuminated mist of rain. The trailer travels slowly, floodwaters obscuring its tires. Then it further transforms, into a vehicle for revelation, when its backside comes into view. They see a young man's sad face pressed against the rear window, and his vivid sorrow penetrates any last vestige of their impasse with healing precision. They want to run out after him and advise him not to live life looking back with such unhappiness.

But the Winnebago trails off and the young man's face disappears. Raj and Chandra turn to one another, staring across a fresh clearing unclaimed by his words or her feelings.

museum peace

DRAGGING A FISTFUL of black garbage bags—dark membranes trilling the floodwater's surface—Lukas Thalburg slogs toward the Thalburg Historical Museum, determined to salvage Woodhaven's past. Mud sucks hungrily on his boots, and each effort-laden step toward the museum exacts an incremental toll from his middle-aged thighs.

Already breathless mere yards beyond his moored boat, he pauses to rest and vows privately to begin the exercise regimen his cardiologist prescribed years ago. He looks to the museum, trying to envision the now-submerged flagstone path leading to its entrance, his feet searching in vain for its once-dependable guidance.

When he reaches the base of the stairway, he pauses again and waits for his hamstrings to unknot. But when he mounts the lowermost stair, a renegade rush of river cuffs his knees. His legs buckle and he teeters backward, thrashing his arms. The bags within his grasp inflate, pulling him off balance. Reflexively, he unclenches his fists and releases the wind-socked bags before plunging into the water. His heels bang violently against the stairs while he tries to regain an upright position.

He reemerges, gasping for air, and instinctively reaches for the bags in which he had hoped to cull the museum's trove. But already they are beyond retrieval, floating like bloated corpses at a rapidly expanding distance. "Son of a bitch!" he curses, watching them bob past the museum's "Visitors Welcome!" sign.

Now he questions the point of struggling up the stairs to his mother's museum if he cannot carry out its history. He looks between his boat and the museum, trying to choose between them, his skin chafing, his heels throbbing with incipient bruises, unidentifiable debris clinging to his denim jacket.

While he weighs a decision to leave, the sun rips through the gray cloudsheet. It converts the valley's floodwater into a polished mirror that reflects the sky and darting shadows of restive birds. Raindrops glisten like sequins, and windbursts make treetops whistle. For a moment, the strange beauty of it all transports him out of his wretchedness.

But then, as abruptly as it had appeared, the sun retreats and the sky reforms into a solid gray blanket. Rain again falls dully onto the lusterless landscape. Lukas looks down at the opaque floodwater encircling his thighs, appearing to amputate his legs above his knees. The spectacle makes him feel vertiginous, and he urgently fixes his sight on his mother's museum in hopes of steadying himself. But his vertigo merely worsens as he stares at her homage to a town that was founded on a gelatin recipe.

Still, it is now or never to attempt any salvage before the insistent flood destroys the entire museum. In quick desperation, he marshals his resolve, ascends the stairs, and struggles to push open the museum's door against the contrary weight of the flood pressing against it. Finally succeeding, he pauses in the doorway and begins to absorb the watery remapping of the world he had inhabited with his mother decades before.

Stepping guardedly inside, he feels oddly possessed. As though being compelled by someone else's past and their alien urges. He walks automatically to his mother's old desk and stands squarely inside the museum.

At first, the museum is only a vague interior of rippling shadows. He waits for his vision to adjust to the darkness, meanwhile estimating the number of years that have passed since Thalburg Gelatin last rolled off any conveyor belt in Woodhaven. But he finds it painful to wonder about that, because it immediately reminds him about the local residents turning on his mother after she closed the factory during the War.

He tries to refocus, but the unique power of this place to draw him into the past is overwhelming. He cannot fend off thoughts about his parents and his mother's friend, Olivia. Or the pivotal day that Olivia and his father disappeared, leaving his mother stuck forever within her interminable unhappiness behind the curator's desk. And leaving him to watch helplessly while she stared blankly at the fireplace for hours every day, holding on for decades to a museum that mostly catered to lost tourists.

He regrets not knowing his mother in her happier days, before he was born, before the factory closed. It had always been difficult to believe the stories he often heard about his mother's great liveliness before the War. How she loved to throw parties at the factory to celebrate occasions large and small. How she routinely rallied people around civic issues or charity drives. And how she sponsored an annual gelatin festival that drew contestants from all of California.

Finally, the museum's shadows yield to gradients of darkness, enhancing his perception of shapes and distance. Words in the banner above the desk become visible: "Welcome to the Thalburg Historical Museum—The *Original* Home of Thalburg Gelatin!"

Lukas examines his mother's desk, wondering what remains so many years after the museum's closure. There's the vibrantly painted diorama that the Rodriguez family donated—a parade of wagons and human figurines, carrying fruit baskets and flowers to market. The tarnished brass lamp with its cracked glass hood. A motley assortment of fountain pens inside a war bonds cup. The clay replica of a Thalburg Gelatin carton that he made during art class eons ago.

He rummages through the drawers, finding barnacled paperclips, stiff rubber bands, stacks of coasters from a Los Angeles hotel . . . There's a rusty key—*to what?*—that he pockets for himself.

Using his flashlight, he walks to the windows and draws back the curtains. Columns of muted sun enter the museum, and the interior displays begin to scavenge the newly available light. White objects rush into view, and he sees the pale round rim of the wall clock, ivory doorknobs, ceiling smoke alarms, a floating lampshade. Then objects that split light with their striped or checkerboard patterns emerge: the Dunleavys' Celtic coat of arms, the checkered tile trim around the windowsills, the barber pole from Mr. Bertolli's shop. Finally, all the darkly colored objects materialize, revealing the full extent of the museum's visible devastation.

He feels seasick taking inventory of the historical displays that are now all unmoored or sundered into parts that levitate eerily on the floodwaters. A papier-mâché bust of Woodhaven's first mayor floats facedown, butting against a wall. The "Thalburg Pyramid"—an historic collection of cartons that packaged Thalburg Gelatin—has collapsed, and its Sphinx head is floating inside the fireplace cove. A life-sized mannequin, attired in a Thalburg factory workers' uniform, drifts like an aloof casualty near Juliette Williams' homage to Rosa Parks. A cardboard totem created by first-graders in 1943 to represent gelatin manufacture has nearly dissolved: the cow has warped into amorphous cellulite, the pig has transformed into a new species, and the chicken headpiece has lost its painted eyes to the wash of the flood.

A sunflash ricochets off the cherrywood display cabinet that Tomasz Podroski built. Lukas looks to its cache of winning recipes from the annual Thalburg Cooking Contests, won routinely by Tomasz's wife Annie or her friend, Tess McCracken.

Adjacent bookcases shelve the town's historical documents and local authors' works—all beyond rescue. Ella Strather's self-published eulogy, "Woodhaven, Our Proud Town" . . . Akiko Dunleavy's "Love Haikus from the Canyon" and "Reflections on the Baptista River" . . . Raj Joshipura's many editorials in the *Woodhaven Courier* . . . scrapbooks containing archival records about Thalburg Gelatin. He startles when he spots above the bookcase the framed adage that his mother and Olivia concocted one day:

To study the evolution

of packaging and advertisements for

Thalburg Gelatin

is to come to understand

the history of modern American.

Throughout his adulthood, he has often found himself mindlessly reciting those plodding words. Seeing them now in their original inscription recalls the day they were concocted. He remembers playing with toy soldiers on an orange rug in front of the fireplace while his mother and Olivia shared lunch and juggled various arrangements of words. He remembers them bursting into laughter once they finally conceived this "perfect arrangement," and then sliding off the desk to join in a celebratory dance. His mother's blue shoes tapped the floor, and Olivia's flaming red curls bounced with her steps. Then they pulled him into their silly dance, his plastic soldiers dropping to the rug.

And . . . still. Still, how to reconcile such a terrible next day, so joyless in comparison, when his father and Olivia disappeared? How to understand why they left him and his mother behind?

He has spent decades with the mystery of their disappearance claiming his attention and dreams. Clues have been wanting, and what little he can recall of the terrible day yields only context with uncertain meaning. Arriving with his mother at Olivia's cottage only to find a stranger who answered the door. Later coming home, and his father gone, too. Then his mother vanishing behind a veil of obscure sorrow, becoming forever fixed in her long somber stare toward the fireplace.

Lukas withdraws his father's German prayer book from a top shelf of the bookcase. He flips through its thumb-worn pages, cursing his father for his ungodly behavior. Blaming him for his mother's devitalizing loneliness. For Olivia's disappearance. For consigning him to a childhood filled with numbing absences.

And just as mysterious, he still can't understand how his father—such a cold, duplicitous man—continued to earn his mother's longing, let alone seduce Olivia. And Olivia's betrayal of his mother—how could she have so convincingly feigned their friendship for so long?

He pitches his father's prayer book into the flood-water and says, "Good riddance, old man." But the symbolic burial provides mere momentary respite from the insistently impinging past. Because when he walks to the fireplace and glances back toward his mother's desk, he instantly re-enters her old annihilating stare. Her lifeless gaze clutches him, pulls him back through time, reconfigures him to the past. He instantly feels extraneous and indistinct, dimly perceived in her eyes.

But what he can also see now—his woeful inheritance of his mother's unlived life, and his lifelong compulsion to mirror her sorrowful outlook. At the same revelatory moment, he experiences perverse consolation, reconnecting to his mother through the only feeling she had to offer him.

Driven by instinct, he imagines himself looking defiantly back at his mother and, as a self-preserving act, resisting the power of her gaze to extinguish him. His grief acutely expands while he registers all the years he has misspent living his subliminal life.

It does not help when he finally turns away and incidentally sees his face reflected in the floodwaters, looking back so indistinctly. He curses its mockery and angrily kicks it, but he loses footing again. He reaches for the fireplace mantel, but the brick he grabs comes loose and even weights his fall.

He is still cursing when he reemerges, removing odd debris from his forehead, spitting something sour out of his mouth. Noting the brick in his hand, he looks curiously to the fireplace and sees a new cavity in its cove where the brick had been. The river slips in and out of the cavity, performing tricks with water and light that cause its mortar shell to sparkle. He reaches inside and finds a small cedar box that he sets on the mantle. Then he carefully unclasps its rusted latch and opens the lid.

Inside the box is a faded blue envelope, a necklace, and crumbled remnants of a pale flower. When he withdraws the necklace, he sees a heart-shaped locket that is inscribed: "To Claire. Love, always."

With renewed contempt, he again rails against his traitorous father. "Yeah, 'always'—at least until you began screwing her best friend." Then he flings the locket against a wall—it cracks and drops into the floodwater. And repulsed to discover that it was to this relic that his mother had always stared, he shouts, "She trusted you, you cheating bastard! And you broke her!"

He grabs the blue envelope. It bears neither a postmark nor a return, but it is addressed in cursive longhand, "To Mrs. Claire Thalburg."

Anticipating further evidence of his father's infidelity, he withdraws the letter and reads:

May 5, 1959
My Dearest Claire,

My agony has become intolerable. I feel nothing but despair.

You remain my one love, my greatest joy. But in truth, I realize now that our love is not enough for you, and that it causes you terrible pain. I can no longer bear to be the reason for it.

Shocked to uncover any hint of tenderness in his father, Lukas is compelled to reread those sentences. It is confounding to imagine that his father's leaving might have been motivated by an intention to alleviate his mother's suffering. His once-solid view of his parents' lives begins to bend under the weight of new doubt. His mind reels as he reads on:

I trust you understand why I must leave. Each time I see you with Lukas, I die a little more, reminded of the possibilities that life denies us both.

But I accept now that you and I will never live our lives fully together. And in the hours since you've made your decision, I have made mine. I cannot stay and inflict more suffering on you.

I hope my leaving frees you from your dilemma. Remember me when the morning glories bloom.

I will love you always.
Forever yours.

Lukas rests his head on the mantle while his life continues to break free from the illusions that have sustained it. It had been unthinkable before—that his father was capable of such passion or noble sentiment. That his leaving might have been complicated by suffering of his own. That his abandonment could have been more than a purely selfish act.

But now he wonders—if there'd been such seeming mutual longing between his parents, why were they so incapable of staying together? Of pulling each other through whatever hardships they were facing, regardless of what may have transpired between Olivia and his father? How had his mother not taken the opportunity, suggested in the letter, to convince his father to stay so that the three of them could continue as a family, repairing their lives over time?

Sorrow floods his heart. He has wasted so much of his life in such muddled fictions about his family. He has foolishly spent years with counterfeit feelings and beliefs. His one precious life has been a futile attempt to decode his mother's sorrow and his father's absence, and he failed miserably at both.

Rain pelts the museum's darkening windows, and Lukas notes the lateness of the hour. He gathers himself for the trek back to his boat, scanning his mother's devastated museum one final time.

Claiming the letter as the only relic he will salvage from the museum, he grabs the blue envelope from the mantle and turns away. But something tumbles out. And once again, his world is violently overturned as yet another piece of truth shatters his construction of the past. A tuft of red hair, like a wing of fire, drifts down and alights on the floodwater.

⌐ dying to tell ⌐

IT'S NOT TRUE, the old saying that "the dead have no tales to tell." In fact, we dead communicate *all* the time. And the people we've left behind listen for us, with varying degrees of faith and doubt. You know that. In fact, you are hearing me now and, perhaps, contemplating what I've just said.

I have one tale to tell that forever matters to me now. But before I tell it, I want to provide a preface of sorts, by way of passing on two pieces of information I wish I had possessed while I was alive.

One—you should know that when you die, you do not finally discover "the great meaning of life." I realize that may disappoint you. Perhaps it is something you don't wish to hear. But take it from me—it is a fact.

Two—the most ironic thing of all is that, after you die, you exist forever within the meaning you made of your life *while* you lived. So, you see, you discover there is only "life"—no real "after-life" at all.

These discoveries shocked me.

Years ago, just before I died, I remember hoping that, at the very least, my death would free me from my perpetual longing and from my unending struggle with truth and love. I was hoping that the great white light, rumored to appear at death, would at the same time illuminate an understanding of my difficult life. And I was praying to be forgiven for my misguided sensibilities that had inflicted so much damage—on my son Lukas, my husband, and my Olivia.

But when I literally shifted out of life and into death, nothing much happened. No white light, no music. No welcoming spirits or divine absolution. I simply exited life with my inner being intact. My body just peeled off and stayed behind.

And now, I am fixed forever as the person I chose to be in life, and I can't change a thing.

So, as was true while I was alive, my experience in eternity remains bracketed—by my flawed version of truth on one side, and by my flawed version of love on the other. And I remain unable to make those two meet. I abide forever in doubt and loneliness, fixed in my great longing for Olivia.

Olivia Beaumont. Her luminous green eyes. Her flaming red hair caressing her porcelain face. The way her soft lips rolled words in a sweet southern drawl that drew me like honey. I thought I loved her completely then. But now, unburdened by the distractions of bodies and the great fear I carried about our so-called illicit desire, I love her even more.

My son Lukas was a quiet and vague sort of boy who grew into a sulking, opaque man, slow of heart and quick to anger. I know I am to blame, and I remain deeply regretful. When he was a child, I was only marginally available to him. I wanted to be more accessible, but . . . I couldn't. I was battling full-time with depression after Olivia and my husband left. And I spent years waiting for their returns. But I only waited in the end. And while I waited, I made even more grievous errors with my son.

So . . . my husband. He was a remote man of rigid principles who showed his emotions sparingly, even to me in our best of times together. We operated a farm that sprawled across the valley between the East and West Ridge hills. Our house hugged a creek that often tripled in size during rainy seasons that fed the Baptista.

We also owned the gelatin factory. It supplied jobs for many Woodhaven residents and for an annual influx of migrant workers, many of whom stayed and later became neighbors. The factory and the farm kept us very busy.

But then World War II arrived, and it tore us all apart. Everything good ultimately unraveled. And most of the ruin was my fault.

I was wrong—I know that now—but during the War, I believed I could save my husband's family from the concentration camps, using money from the sale of our gelatin manufacturing rights. A large Midwestern food conglomerate had made a good offer, but my husband forbade me to sell. He insisted that the Nazis would only steal our money and end up killing his parents and brothers anyway. Still, I felt I had to try. I believed that a bribe provided the only hope of saving them.

So, I closed the factory after selling the rights to Thalburg Gelatin to a Kansas food-processing company. I smuggled the proceeds from the sale to my sister, Aimee, who lived in Paris. She used them to bribe a consul for his promise to free my husband's family from Buchenwald and arrange their emigration to America. For weeks, I waited for word that they were on a ship bound for New York.

But months passed. And then a year. And we never saw his family again. In the end, we lost our factory and most of our savings, and many people in Woodhaven lost jobs.

My husband became completely cold toward me then. Not a bitter or vengeful cold that, at least, would have let me know that I could still somehow affect him emotionally. Instead, his was a lifeless and numb sort of cold that I could not sway. And that is how I became lost to my husband—at least, for the first time.

Then, my son Lukas . . . I gave birth to him several years later. That was an absolute miracle. My husband and I hadn't had sex in nearly a decade and, as it turned out, we would never have it again. Lukas was born during an inexplicable momentary lapse of my husband's coldness.

So . . . after we—that is, after I—lost the factory, I carried on as curator of the Thalburg Historical Museum which my husband and I had founded during our happier days. But, as might well be expected, many neighbors turned against us after losing their factory jobs. And my life in Woodhaven became even lonelier.

Still, the museum provided me with something to do, and it served as a tourist attraction for the occasional out-of-town visitor. And later, importantly, it provided a safe place where Olivia and I could meet.

We met at the museum most afternoons. It's hard to account for all the hours we spent together, so much of it simply staring at one another, talking about everything and nothing. Whenever she smiled at me, I would feel her eyes penetrate my soul, and their brightness seemed to project from a place within her heart where she steadfastly envisioned the possibility of our lives together. In those moments, we often mutually imagined ourselves living in a different place and time, touching each other, holding each other close, caressing, kissing. But we only did such things in our minds back then, because we didn't trust the world to tolerate physical expressions of our love.

Meanwhile, my husband labored to maintain the farm. But he was ruined by his disappointment in me and his grief over losing his family. Our fields slowly withered from neglect and barely sustained us. The strawberry vines and apple trees shriveled on the outskirts of our property, creating a sad dark boundary around the farm. Rows of broccoli and cauliflower contracted into hard brown scars. Sweet peas and golden zucchini rotted unceremoniously on trellises. Sometimes, when I'd come home from the museum,

I'd find my husband sitting lifeless on the porch, like a heavy stone in the center of all that barrenness.

I grew increasingly anxious about his deepening depression, watching helplessly as he continued to wander through his anesthetized life. And, of course, I felt responsible because of my betrayals—first, with me selling the factory. And second, with my heart—with Olivia.

Olivia begged me not to tell my husband about us. But at a point when he had become so lifelessly withdrawn, I risked trying to save him by telling him the truth. I decided to cast aside all deception because I understood how deception had destroyed him—my duplicity in losing our factory, and the Nazis' awful deceit. I believed then that my husband may have needed truth as an antidote to his anesthesia, a serum that could revive him. I felt I owed him that much.

But Olivia kept insisting otherwise. She said that telling him about us would only serve my selfish need to relieve my guilty conscience. And she pointed out that it would jeopardize the fragile arrangement we had struck to accommodate our love. She believed the news would destroy him, and that I was mistaken to think that truth and love were always compatible or required. "Neither your husband nor the world needs to know about us," she insisted.

She fell silent when I disagreed. And for minutes, nothing sounded but for the alarm in my heart. All the while that Olivia stared at me in disbelief, I watched the light in her eyes extinguish. And when that happened, I felt my future darken. Finally, she suggested that, by leaving Woodhaven, she could free me of my dilemma and my need to tell my husband about our relationship. She believed that her leaving would spare my husband and son from the collateral hazards of the truth I intended to tell about love. I begged her not to go.

Later that night, we spoke on the phone—the last time, as it turned out, that I'd ever hear her voice. I confirmed my decision to tell my husband, and I tried to convince her to stay.

And truthfully—I did not for a moment believe she would leave me. I really didn't think that she *could*.

But within an hour or so of that call, I began to worry that I was wrong. I stayed awake the entire night, wrestling with truth and love, but I kept returning to the necessity of Olivia above anything else. By dawn, I was convinced that I could not live without her. And I realized that telling my husband about us would only destroy the compromised claims on happiness that each of us could ever hope to have. Love and truth, I finally decided, would have to suffer concessions for everyone's sake.

I could barely wait for the morning to set out with Lukas for Olivia's cottage and tell her in person about my new clarity of mind. So, I woke my son early and fed him a hasty breakfast. And together, we rushed along the footpaths toward Olivia's cottage. But—as I would later discover—by the time we had travelled halfway to her home, Olivia was already driving to our house to deliver a message of her own. While Lukas and I were crossing a felled redwood that bridged the Baptista, Olivia was placing a blue envelope in our mailbox. And as I knocked on her cottage door—me so eager to tell her how I had reconciled my conflict with love and truth—my husband was opening the blue envelope and discovering the letter and locket it contained. When a strange woman answered Olivia's door and told me about Olivia's departure, my husband had begun packing his suitcase. When I returned home within the hour, reeling in agony over Olivia's exile, I discovered that my husband had left me as well. He wrote no note of his own. But, tellingly, he placed Olivia's letter and locket on our bed.

Throughout the decades that followed, I waited for Olivia and my husband to come back to me. I was prepared to accept any imperfections in truth and love that were required for their return. I just wanted them back in my life.

So . . . I maintained the museum. I figured that Olivia and my husband could always locate me there if they ever wanted. But, as I've said, in the end I simply waited. I waited for them for the rest of my life. I filled time by dreaming the inner landscape where Olivia and I had loved one another, and by atoning for the suffering I caused my husband.

Like the objects I kept in the museum, my life, I know, will be viewed through different perspectives by different onlookers over time. And, in short order, it will be forgotten all together. Until then, official records attest to my existence—as wife, mother, daughter of Austrian immigrants, the inventor of edible gelatin, a museum curator, a factory owner in Woodhaven, California. Those durable facts will form a sturdy visible shell encasing my actual life, the one you are hearing about now.

I believe that the legacy of my longing ruined my son and made him inadequate of heart. But back

when he was a child, during all the times I sat waiting at my desk while he played in front of the fireplace, I was never certain what to tell him about my
life, about his father's leaving, and about Olivia.

And even now, if I had the chance to talk with
him, I still wouldn't know how to explain it all. I
remain unimpressed with the power of facts to por-
tray my life, and I don't trust love's telling to convey
it any better.

⌐ daily bread ⌐

JULIETTE LEFT THE BAR a couple of hours ago. She
wanted to say goodbye one last time before leaving
tomorrow for her sister's retirement community in
Berkeley. She wasn't . . . let's say, "happy," to find Ella
here with me. My god—those two! They've had such
a strained relationship. And for *fifty years!* It's been
exhausting to watch them bump up against each other
all that time. I suppose you have to give them points
for stamina. Still—what good are points in such a
pointless battle?

Anyhow, Juliette maintained her usual composure
when she saw Ella packing liquor cartons for me. And
Ella, as usual, remained on edge. Each of them mus-
tered an obligatory smile and forged through custom-

ary awkwardness. And they kept their usual distance from each other.

Then Juliette joined me at the bar, sitting down on the same stool she took when she first set foot in Olivia's decades ago. She made the same old private joke, addressing me as "Miss Olivia." We laughed, but only halfheartedly. Because I was feeling how badly I was going to miss her. I told her so, and that just started us both crying.

Like old times, I poured us each a couple fingers of tequila. We clinked our glasses and said what we always said whenever we raised a toast: "To Olivia." After finishing our shots, she had to hurry home to finish packing. We agreed to meet at the evacuation center early in the morning to say a few more goodbyes together.

All the while we talked, I saw Ella in the background, trying hard not to pay us too much attention. But she has always been intrigued by the intimacy between Juliette and me. I think she actually studies us sometimes, looking for clues to explain our friendship in hopes of understanding the impossibility of theirs.

I am not well-schooled, and I don't pretend to know half of what Ella knows about psychology from her extensive reading and television viewing. But, in my humble opinion? Her main problem with the three of us is her fear of making a mistake with Juliette. She speaks to Juliette in overly contrived ways, trying to manage her uncertainty. She strategizes conversations ahead of time instead of letting them unfold naturally. It seems that Ella keeps trying to figure out "the correct" way to talk to a person who is black, so she keeps on missing a genuine conversation with the person who is Juliette.

Of course, Juliette never helps matters much. She never tries to create opportunities for either of them to risk a different experience of the other. And she seems heavily invested in Ella remaining the very same person who approached her in my bar a very long time ago.

To me, the craziest thing about their situation is that neither of them realizes how much they need the other to preserve a deep personal sense of themselves. The identity they each cling to depends on the other's remaining intact. Ella's experience of Juliette's difference fuels her constant neediness to connect with other people. And Juliette's experience of Ella's difference reliably confirms a sense of otherness that she wants to hang onto.

Juliette and I also share a special connection because of our relationships with Olivia. Each of us discovered a way to survive through living out parts of her life—Juliette in Olivia's cottage, and me in Olivia's bar.

I met Olivia just a few weeks after she opened the bar. My husband Frank had recently died in the War, somewhere on the outskirts of the Black Forest—just two months and eight days after he joined the infantry. I had begged him not to enlist, but he was convinced it was "the right thing to do." He believed the fight against Hitler was a moral imperative, and he was prepared to put his life on the line for his convictions. He even lied about his bad back to qualify for service.

I understood his perspective. And yet, it also mattered to me that we were newlyweds. That we had plans for a family, a garden, a future together. His decision to go overseas and fight a foreign war . . . well, it didn't sound right enough to me in our particular circumstances. Besides, we were new to Woodhaven and didn't know a soul. So, his leaving meant that I'd be alone, also fending for myself in foreign territory. I just wanted to believe that he felt equally compelled by a conviction to live the life we had planned together.

I knew he loved me, but he seemed to be prioritizing his *ideas* about democracy and freedom over the importance of my very real hand inside his every day. It felt wrong for the "us" in flesh-and-blood to lose out to such abstractions. Still, I knew he would lose all self-respect if he didn't enlist. And that began to feel not quite right enough to me. So, in the end, I reluctantly accepted his decision, and I tried not to make him feel guilty about leaving me.

After he died, I felt his absence in very real, very particular, very tangible ways. No abstractions comforted me in the least. None of his cherished ideals or convictions made any heartening sense. "Democracy" without the choice of us living our lives together? Peace for what purpose? Freedom to do exactly what? Justice for whom?

I had no peace. I felt no freedom. I experienced no justice. Two months and eight days' worth of his self-respect was not worth losing a lifetime together.

When we moved to Woodhaven, we parked our small house trailer in the secluded backwoods behind the West Ridge hills, hoping to evade anyone's notice or demand for rent. We had little money after the purchase of our trailer. And the gelatin factory jobs that we had expected had become suddenly unavailable.

The day Frank left for the War . . . I close my eyes now and can still see him in his uniform, waving goodbye in the doorway of our trailer. So young and handsome, with his curly brown hair, his sparkling blue eyes . . . That day . . . He told me not to worry. He promised he'd come back to me. But he never did.

Even after his sister from Arizona miraculously located me and informed me of his death, I stayed inside our trailer, waiting for him to fulfill his promise. I rarely left our bed. I lost interest in the world and any appetite for what it might have to offer. Within weeks, my clothes began to droop, and I got soft in the head. I was not the least bit right enough.

But then one morning, I thought I heard someone knock on the trailer door. It took a while to figure out that it wasn't one of my hallucinations about Frank returning home. I slowly got out of bed and opened the door. It blinded me, all the sunlight pouring in. I couldn't see much at first. But I thought I heard someone—or something—rushing away through the tall grasses that had overtaken our trailer. When my vision readjusted, I saw a wicker basket on the front step. It contained a loaf of bread and a jar of jam.

I stared at the basket a while before carrying it inside. Then I set it down on the wooden crate that Frank and I had used for a dining table. I hesitated to open it because, frankly, I didn't think I had the energy or interest to eat.

And yet, when I touched that loaf of rye, something mysterious happened. I swear, I felt the hands that made it. And they were warm and strong and comforting. I tore off a small piece of bread and placed it in my mouth, and I felt communion. I dipped my finger into the strawberry jam and ran it across my lips. I have never tasted such sweetness since.

Days passed, and the baskets kept appearing on my doorstep. They often contained surprises—ripe oranges, chunks of cured ham, pastry wrapped in wax paper twisted at the ends. And once, near Christmas, I found a ceramic baby Jesus inside a small crib.

Over time, I regained strength. I started making forays to a nearby creek off the Baptista to wash my hair and teeth.

Finally, I awoke one day and decided to rinse my good dress in that creek. After it dried, I put it on and set out on the path that had been smoothed through the grass fields by the strangers who had been travelling to my doorstep with their baskets. And as I walked that same path back toward them, I realized that I had been saved.

The path led to a wooden shack alongside a filling station on a dirt road. But I found no one there. And though I was shy about talking to anyone after weeks of isolation, I walked up to the shack and peered through its front window. I will never forget what I saw. Its walls were plastered with pictures of saints, and votive candles suspended from the ceiling by chains. Religious statues cluttered the bookshelves. And there was a nativity set on top of a TV—with its baby Jesus missing!

My surprise turned to shock when, out of nowhere, Ed Utley appeared, staring at me with his impish grin. He told me to hop on the back of his motorcycle, and then he drove me up the hill to Olivia's. I felt like I was hopping into a dream.

He accompanied me into the bar, and that's when I first saw Olivia. She was gorgeous, like a model, with a fiery shock of red hair. While she tended the bar, she displayed a strength and authority that you rarely observed in women those days. When she turned her attention on me, she seemed to take me in instantly. With one look and few words, she sat me down and gave me water and food. Then she offered me a job in exchange for my keep. And that is precisely when I decided that I wanted to live.

I swept Olivia's several times a day, even when that wasn't necessary. I shined the wineglasses and flatware every night. In the afternoons, I chopped vegetables for the stew pot. And each week, I washed and ironed the checkered tablecloths. Olivia even taught me how to mix cocktails and serve them "proper Southern style."

Within months, she was comfortable leaving me alone to tend the bar while she spent her afternoons at the Thalburg Museum with her friend, Claire. I never asked her about that friendship because I saw how happy she was whenever she returned from the museum. And that was all I needed to know. When patrons offered their worthless speculations about Olivia and Claire's relationship, I would simply cut them off. Because I knew what it was like to love someone like that, only to lose them to an abstraction or ideology.

I was shocked the day she told me that she'd be leaving Woodhaven within the week. Her decision seemed rash and mysterious, and I wanted to understand. I wanted to help her like she had helped me.

And, of course, I also recognized the despair. Her eyes looked lifeless, and I imagined they were seeing what I had seen so many years before: the benumbing seduction of death. I tried to give her hope. I reminded her about what had happened to me—strangers with bread baskets, new paths appearing out of nowhere and leading to unfathomed possibilities of friendship and community. I wanted her to believe she could survive a shattered heart. And, selfishly, I didn't want to lose our friendship.

But Olivia refused to discuss the reasons for her hasty departure. She said that, while she couldn't explain her troubles, she trusted that I understood well enough. Then, knowing I was penniless, she offered me Olivia's for the promise of keeping its name. I resisted, but she just handed me a keepsake bottle of champagne, shook my hand and said goodbye.

The next day, Juliette drove into town—dispirited and lost, needing a place to stay. So, I was happy to think that I might help Olivia in some small way. I asked Juliette to wait at the counter while I phoned Olivia—even though she had made me promise not to call. Fortunately, she was grateful for my suggestion that Juliette rent her cottage while she was gone, to wherever she was going, for however long.

As it turned out, Olivia left Woodhaven two days after that. And Juliette has lived in her cottage ever since.

But it took weeks before Juliette first ventured out. She didn't even answer the phone at first. Still, I kept calling, just to let her know that someone kept her in mind.

Then one day, she dropped by the bar unannounced and acted as though her visit was the most unremarkable thing in the world. She asked for a shot of tequila. It was great to see her like that. I poured us each a couple of fingers, and we raised our glasses. Spontaneously, we each said, "To Olivia." And that's how our traditional toast began near fifty years ago.

Over those next five decades, Ella often asked me to explain the "secret" of my friendship with Juliette. Sometimes I tried, hoping to ease her distress. I would explain how we'd been drawn together, each of us having suffered the loss of a husband that left us paralyzed by life-stopping grief. And the kinship we also shared, by having made it through those tough times in Olivia's spirit. But my explanations never satisfied her.

Just before Juliette left the bar tonight, we promised to visit one another in our future homes. She gave me her sister's address—for the umpteenth time. And I again gave her the phone number of the motel where I'd be staying while figuring out whether to come back to Woodhaven and reopen the bar. Then she stood up and waved goodbye to Ella who was rearranging boxes on shelves.

I was expecting that, as usual, Ella would walk over to Juliette, and a stiff hug would pass between them. And I was prepared to watch over them, as usual, so they could experience me holding them somehow together.

But what I actually saw? They did not approach one another. They did not hug. Instead, Ella stayed at the rear of the bar and looked directly back at Juliette. They stared at each other a moment or two, and, finally, Juliette picked up her umbrella and walked out the door.

And as sad as it was to see—with such thudding finality—that they'd never succeeded in forging a path between them, it was also a relief. Finally, it seemed, they had acknowledged the genuine distance between them, without protest or blame. And as late as it was in our lives for any major epiphany like that, it was most definitely all right enough by me.

$\backsim$ lost and found $\sim$

ROSIE'S EGG-SHAPED EYE FALLS from its socket and lands sunny-side-up on her furry knee.

Grace witnesses the horror, her own eyes expanding with the shock of it all. She quickly retrieves her stuffed monkey's fallen eye and wipes it clean against her T-shirt. "Oh, Rosie," she exclaims sympathetically, "you can't see with your knee." She kisses the flat emptied socket on Rosie's forehead and flips over the renegade eye. After spitting onto its metallic backside, she explains, "You need *two* eyes on your *head,* so you can see right." She swirls the saliva with her index finger until a gluey slur forms, and then she returns the eye to its socket, pushing it hard into Rosie's forehead. For a brief, cheery moment, Rosie is re-sighted.

But when Grace steps back to admire her handi-work, the eye droops and dangles eerily off matted strands of Rosie's orange fur. Sighing dramatically, Grace resets the eye and presses her thumbs against it, this time transmitting the entire weight of her body through her hands. But the force proves exces-sive; Rosie's eye buckles and snaps and drops again to the ground. Grace looks down at the crumpled coin of eye and cries, "Rosie, I'm sorry! I broke your eye."

It is so painful to endure. Already, this day has earned status as *the* worst day of Grace's life, despite there having been plenty of others to compete.

Grace reminds herself that she must remain strong to make it through difficult times like the present. That is what her parents always tell her, even though they are divorced—a fact that seems to suggest to Grace that they do not follow their own advice.

But it is hard to feel strong and self-confident in light of the day's foreboding events, especially while she stands on the riverbank now and registers how enormous the Baptista River is becoming. In the past, it was only a series of small creeks that trickled across her front yard. Now it is one huge body of water wreaking havoc on everyone she loves. *How do things like this just happen?*

She notices Rosie's staid and uncomplaining ex-pression (even after losing an eye!). And, considering that resilient spirit, she feels ashamed about her own ill-temper and self-doubt. She tenderly commends Rosie, "You're such a brave monkey. And you're being such a good girl about all of this."

Inspired by Rosie's exemplary courage, Grace picks up the fractured eye and determines to fix it. She places it on a river rock and, after finding the perfect stone, tries to hammer it flat. But she whacks it once, twice, three times before realizing that she has inadvertently scratched off the white of the rogue eye, exposing steely tracks of gray undercoating.

Now, despite her earnest efforts to remain calm, she cannot stop herself from crying. She looks into Rosie's one good eye and, hoping to offer comfort, whispers, "Daddy will know how to fix this." She picks up Rosie and carefully positions her on the trunk of a nearby felled redwood. She says, "You just relax here and watch the sky for our angels."

Grace unfurls her father's sleeping bag on the ground below Rosie's perch, under a small tarp that deflects the mizzly rain filtering through a canopy of tree branches. She resolves to obtain good rest tonight because tomorrow she and Rosie must leave at dawn to begin settlement into their new life.

Peering back at her house, Grace feels a modicum of guilt. It is not so easy to abandon her mother there all alone, knowing what will likely become of her. Still, she knows she does not want to join her self-destructive mother in a suicidal drowning. Besides, as her parents often claimed—especially when she posed questions about their divorce—she was "too young for many things." And death—it seems to her—must be one of those "things."

She is not surprised by her mother's manifest incompetence in dealing with this flood. But it is hard to understand why her father is not here protecting them. It makes no sense that he would leave her in such dire straits, in the unreliable hands of her mother. Did he really go back to Michigan today, as her mother claims?

But the phones aren't working, the roads are washed out, and even Mrs. Strather hasn't dropped by today to lecture her mother (yet again) about her parental duties and the urgent need to evacuate. There's no one to help Grace fend against her mother's insistent strategy to remain in the house during the flood. She looks at her father's sleeping bag, stares at its depressing flatness, and wishes he were inside of it, staying close to her tonight.

Dusk begins to infuse the sky, intensifying the prevailing gloom. Grace switches on her flashlight, sets it on the sleeping bag, and aims its beam on the shoebox she has filled with rations. "Rosie," she says, trying to sound reassuring, "we got everything we need."

But then the Baptista growls like a hungry monster's stomach, and her fragile resolve falters. The creek-turned-river sounds louder than it has ever sounded before, through all the many nights she has camped here with her father on the outskirts of their property. Trying to tame her fear, she invokes the memory of her strong father and walks several yards to the newly widened riverbank. Emulating him, she cups one hand over her eyes and scans the Baptista: first upstream toward town, then downstream toward the weathered footbridge. Finally, like him, she breathes in the night air and looks across the river to the big hill, up to where Olivia's sits at the top, and to the indistinct foam of stars capping the canyon.

But everything looks different than before. The Baptista is bloated, as big as an actual river. Only a handful of lights emanate from hillside homes. The footbridge skirts the water's surface. And when she emulates her father's yawn that routinely concludes his authoritative survey of the canyon, she finds herself anxious and afraid instead.

Then her mother's razor-like voice slices through her burgeoning sadness. "Gracie!" it calls from afar.

Grace flinches. She places a finger across her lips to signal Rosie to remain quiet.

"Come home, Gracie Woods," her mother yells. "And I mean *now*," she trails off.

Crouching to escape detection, Grace heads back to her father's sleeping bag. She conceals the flashlight by scooping it up and pressing it into her belly to bury its beam.

"Honey?" her mother beckons in her wobbly voice.

But Grace stays hidden behind the toppled redwood and waits.

"Baby," her mother slurs, "come on home now, won't you?"

From experience, Grace knows that it will not be long before her mother tires. So, she bides her time, staring at the warm circle of light that transilluminates her belly. She moves the flashlight in figures-of-eight across her stomach, absorbing its warmth.

"Damn it, Gracie," her mother complains. "I think it's getting kinda late."

After minutes of silence, Grace risks peeking out from her hideaway. Cautiously, she raises her head above the felled redwood and peers at her mother—a thin, jittery shadow inside a skewed quadrangle of light that flows out the front doorway and across the yard.

Her mother whines, "C'mon, honey. I need my little helper!"

Grace rolls her eyes and hunkers down in her hideout, resigned to stay patient. She listens to screeching crickets and hollow-throated night owls. While trilling the grass with her fingers, she silently recites the alphabet forward and backward. She thinks about her friend, Tommy Nichols, and his magical hand with its six fingers, and she worries that she may never see him again.

Finally, Grace hears her mother's shrill command to "Get back here right now!" It sounds surprisingly vigorous, and Grace's heart thumps. Her mother could be very mean when she was drunk which, nowadays, was every day. During those times, it was just as risky to obey her as it was not to.

Warily, Grace sneaks another glance at the house. She sighs in relief when the quadrangle of light encasing her mother's shadow finally collapses into a bright line that extinguishes when the door slams shut.

"We're safe now," she whispers as she mounts the tree trunk and lies down with Rosie. "And now we can look for angels together. Daddy says that you see them the best when it's the most dark."

Grace knows everything about angels that any human can possibly know. She has watched their stories on television and film. She's studied them on Christmas cards and held long conversations with their statues in church. She has read about them in her favorite picture books. Cherub-faced postage stamps are stuck to her bedposts. Images of angels often float freely through her mind, between her thoughts and across her dreams. She remembers her father's steadfast promise that angels will always watch over her if he is not around to protect her.

She stares into the foamy sky, vigilant for the telling flutter of angel wings. But after what seems to be an eternity, all that appears are a few potent stars that burn pinpoint holes through the clouds. It seems even darker than the night she camped here with her father and counted *one hundred* stars before falling asleep in his lap.

Trying to sustain Rosie's attention, she says, "Angels are stronger than stars, so they can get through the clouds better. Just keep your eye open for them, okay?"

But failing to spot any angels for the time it takes her to sing three complete songs inside her head, Grace falls into an apprehensive mood. She sits up and looks uncertainly toward her mother's house, trying to resist an urge to return to it. Already its window shades are drawn, indicating that her mother probably lingers in the living room, passed out on the sofa. Grace feels empty whenever she imagines her mother like that, so she suggests to Rosie that they eat something.

Heading toward their rations box, Grace sadly recalls the comments she overheard her mother make last week to her latest boyfriend: "My Gracie," her mother had declared, "she just eats and eats and gets bigger all the time!" The new boyfriend did not respond and—like those who'd come before him—seemed disinterested in any discussion concerning Grace. Still, her mother had continued: "I really don't understand it, do you? She must've taken her father's fat genes. Because, I mean . . . honestly, just take a look at *me!*"

She feels even more ashamed when she remembers the man's laugh that followed. It is stuck inside her head like a toothache. She wishes she could wipe it out of her memory, but with something less harmful than what her mother uses to forget.

Grace sits down on the sleeping bag, crosses her legs, and removes the rubber bands that secure the rations box. She withdraws Ritz crackers and a jar of grape jelly, and she repositions her flashlight to illuminate the feast. Layering jelly across three crackers with a spoon handle, she asks Rosie, "Doesn't this look delicious?"

Rosie's silence conveys agreement.

Grace gives her a thumbs-up, and then she slides a cracker into her mouth. She thinks, like her father, that grape jelly always tastes more purple outdoors. When finished with her snack, she licks the jelly off her fingers and shoves the rations aside. She tightens the knots in her pink shoelaces and wiggles into the sleeping bag with Rosie. Facing the sky, she says, "Now let's start looking *really* hard for our angels."

Curling her fingers to form a telescope, Grace again scans the heavens. But the firmament remains unruffled. She worries now that no one is listening for her prayer voice, the one she mostly keeps inside and uses for emergencies. The cool night air begins to irritate her throat, and the dampness of the ground begins to seep into her back. She offers up her physical suffering as a sacrifice, bargaining in return for angels to appear. She sweetens the deal, promising, "If you come to me tonight, I will be good forever."

While waiting for a reply, she is surprised to realize that she is newly able to distinguish gradients of black within the sky. She sees that the night sky is lighter in some places and denser in others—not a solid and immutable backdrop of darkness. And when she looks with even greater scrutiny, she discovers tints of blue and purple within it.

Still, the longer she stares at the sky, the more expansive it becomes and the hazardously smaller she feels. For an unsettling moment, she fears she is shrinking into nothingness. Meanwhile, the night noises become menacing—even though they are the same outdoor noises she and her father always call "bedtime music for angels." Now, however, they neither soothe nor uplift. And the muscular breezes that shake the towering trees only rattle her imagination. The covert movements of nocturnal creatures sound spooky. "Please," she prays, clutching Rosie to her chest, "just *one* angel."

She dabs her tears against Rosie's spongy head and again counsels herself to be brave. But the wait for rescuing angels has become insufferable, and she reconsiders their strategy of escape. She crawls out of the sleeping bag and looks back to her mother's weakly lit house, to the spacious sky vacant of angels, to hapless one-eyed Rosie, and to the sleeping bag that does not contain her father. Everything feels so terribly empty.

Staring contemplatively at the ground, she reviews her mother's account of what her father *supposedly* said earlier today. And now she is certain that he would never move back to Michigan without her and everything they both love—Rosie, these hills, this canyon, their Baptista, their starry sky, their own Motel 3.

She bends down to test the knots in her bright pink shoelaces that glisten in the flashlight's beam. She pulls them taut, regretting again having lost her shoe at the carnival last year. That, she knows, is what broke her family apart and changed everything forever. She apologizes to Rosie, "I'm sorry I made this all happen."

Thinking about that terrible night for the millionth time, she still cannot understand how it also provides her most favorite memory. She tries to console herself by recalling that favorite part now—sitting between her parents in a rocking red gondola, suspended in the sky at the top of the Ferris wheel, everyone laughing. Her parents' bodies pressing against hers, making a "family sandwich." Her mother yelling to Mr. Dunleavy who operated the controls: "Stop, Bill! Bring us down!" But how he just kept looking up at her, grinning and ignoring her pleas. It felt so dangerous and exhilarating at once. She even found herself conspiring with Mr. Dunleavy to amplify her mother's giddiness by swinging her legs more vigorously to rock the booth harder.

It likely would have remained a perfect night had she not later told her father about the prickly burrs clinging to her sock. She realizes now that she should have simply offered up her suffering to the angels and walked uncomplainingly back to the ring-toss booth where her father had won Rosie for her. But the longer she walked, the deeper the burrs penetrated her foot and the more she limped. Finally, her father down knelt to diagnose her predicament. And, after officially declaring that "small porcupines" were biting through her anklet, he began removing the burrs. He asked, "Honey, how did you lose your shoe?"

Grace remembers staring up into his tobacco-brown eyes, seeing twirling teacups above his head and a tilt-a-whirl whirling. She remembers crying so hard that she could barely speak. Finally, she guiltily blurted out, "My shoe fell off in the Ferris wheel!"

"Honey," her father had responded, stroking her wavy black hair, trying to calm her down. "Don't be so upset. It was just a silly tennis shoe!"

But she only sobbed harder, trying to explain. "Mom told me to stop kicking up there! But I didn't listen to her."

"Oh, sweetheart," he kept repeating while drying her eyes with his sleeve and waiting for her breathless rendition of her offense. Finally, she told him about her pink sneaker slipping off while the three of them rocked high on the Ferris wheel, and how it tumbled down through the floodlights and dropped some-where to the ground.

"Gracie, that's not so bad!" he said. "We were all just having fun. Let's go back—you, Rosie, and me—and we'll find your shoe, okay? Maybe Mommy's even won you a prize at that duck gallery she won't leave." Then carried her and Rosie in his strong arms, and they headed back toward the Ferris wheel. While they walked, he told a story about the day *he* lost a *pair* of shoes at a bowling alley in Saginaw, Michigan. "Not one, but *two* shoes, Gracie!" he emphasized. "All daddy had was his dirty old socks to walk home in," he laughed. He tickled Rosie and added, "And my socks were full of holes!"

The Ferris wheel was idled when they arrived, its floodlights turned off. A hand-written note on the entry gate indicated that the operator would be "Back in 10 Minutes." Grace's father set her down and instructed her to wait outside the barrier which he subsequently hurdled. Grace hummed while she watched him sprint toward the Ferris wheel and search the motor casing and grounds for her shoe. But after several minutes, he turned to her and shrugged his shoulders. He upturned his empty hands and flashed his crooked smile (the one that always made her laugh). He said, "Oh well. Looks like someone's gonna get herself a brand new pair of pink sneakers."

He started on his way back to her, but something appeared to startle him. He looked off to one side, and his smile vanished. He told Grace to stay put, and then he bee-lined toward a large canvas tent several yards away. After pausing briefly at its entrance as though listening for clues, he flung open its flaps and everything changed.

Grace watched her father's expression turn strange, into something she'd never seen before. She couldn't tell whether he wanted to scream or cry. Almost instantly, Mr. Dunleavy ran out of the tent, and he wasn't wearing a shirt. His belt trailed behind him like a tail.

Then she heard her mother whimpering all the while that her father paced outside the tent, clenching and unclenching his fists, muttering words she was not meant to hear. Soon, a crowd assembled around the tent, and Mr. Rodriguez placed a steadying hand on her father's shoulder, trying to calm him down. Grace searched in vain for Tommy and his mom. Mrs. Strather glanced at her with a kind of knowing expression that frightened her. Finally, Mrs. Williams appeared and ushered her away, repeating all the while "not to worry."

Grace invokes Mrs. Williams' words now, trying not to worry as she scans her bleak encampment and listens to rain strafe the ground. She strokes Rosie's head and whispers, "Not to worry."

But the dismal circumstances seem to convey contrary advisement. She even wonders if she's being punished finally for disobeying her mother and destroying her family.

She casts her final wishes tonight to the impassive sky. For someone to explain the awful emptiness she feels. To tell what is required of her now to undo her father's leaving and her mother's sickness. To make her understand what could possibly happen inside a tent to cause parents to become enemies and families to fall apart.

After crawling back into her father's sleeping bag, she presses her swollen face against its plush flannel. Within minutes, she drifts toward sleep and enters a dreamy, cartoon landscape. Her legs twitch as she surrenders to the powerful gravity of her deep fatigue. But then harsh upsetting words intrude and echo within her dreamscape. Most are words she has learned from her mother—like, "the Jack D", "fucked up", and "cabernet." They rouse her from her sleep, and she cannot ward them away even when she presses her palms against her ears.

She struggles to return to sleep, obsessively wondering whether it's true—as everyone seems to insist—that no one can answer her questions about what happened inside the tent. Whenever she asks her father, he merely repeats, "It has nothing to do with you, Gracie." Without any further expansion, her mother says only, "People don't understand artists." Mrs. Podroski, whose cookies always make her feel better, consistently offers, "Things often happen between two people that no others can explain." Her teacher simply tells her that he "really can't say."

Now she just feels stressed and overly awake. She rolls onto her side and aimlessly shines her flashlight on the damp ground. Within its oval lightscape, she sees hundreds of black ants marching in a shaky line, like skittery chorus dancers under a spotlight. They scuttle over one other, rushing to some obscure destination in the surrounding darkness. Some ants clamp leaf shards in their slit mouths while others ride in piggyback pairs.

Grace whispers to Rosie, "Tomorrow will be better. You'll see. We'll move into Mrs. Podroski's bakery, and we'll make delicious food, and we'll sell cakes for money." She reminds Rosie of her prior baking experience—how she has helped Mrs. Podroski dust angel wings with powdered sugar and ladle batter into greased muffin tins. She adds, "And I know where she keeps her secret recipes. She told me where to find them."

But her attempts at self-composure fail. And the continuing spectacle of the marching ants agitates her beyond measure. She is disturbed by their automatisms. Their unfaltering regimentation in the midst of her life's chaos even seems spiteful. She glowers at the insect zombies, all behaving identically, performing the same monotonous actions, moving in a single direction, no one out of line. Their collective nonchalance about her grim situation and the fact that she hovers menacingly over them is beyond arrogant.

She joins her index finger and thumb in a pinching gesture that she holds threateningly over the ants. But still, they remain unfazed by her power to decimate them. "You stupid ants!" she yells as she flicks several of them out of line. "See what can happen to you?" she screams as she pinches others to their inky deaths. But recruits instantly materialize, and the robust ant columns reconfigure as though nothing at all had happened.

"What is wrong with you?" she shouts. "Those dead ants were your friends and children!" Bending closer toward them, she shouts, "I could kill all of you!"

Her forceful breath momentarily bends the path of trooping ants, but their taut conga formation immediately reassembles. Grace begins pounding the indifferent insects with her fist, snuffing out more of their lives, accumulating thick black crusts on her hand. Still, they continue their course undisturbed, like a powerful stream of dogged electrons.

"You dumb ants!" she hollers as she exits the sleeping bag and stands over them. "Can't you see that your people are gone?" She positions one foot above them and screams, "If you don't care, then take this!" She slams her pink shoe down hard against the ants, tromping all over them. When other recruits restock the assembly, she stomps harder and harder, and then she starts to sob without knowing why.

Suddenly she steps into mushy ground, forcing her to pause and take stock. She notices that the river has reached further onto the banks and closer to her encampment several yards away. And fearing that she and Rosie could drown if they sleep here tonight, she concedes the greater wisdom of spending the night in her warm, dry bed. She confidently wagers that they could sneak out of the house in the morning before her mother ever awakens.

Heading back to their encampment to share this new strategy, Grace calls out, "We're going home now, Rosie." Nearing their sleeping bag, she adds, "It's just for tonight."

But Rosie is nowhere to be found. No longer in the sleeping bag. Not beside or underneath it.

Fretfully, Grace grabs the flashlight and retraces her steps, searching every spot she has visited—the fallen redwood, the bed of river rocks, the ant exposition. "Rosie," she pleads, "where are you?"

But all she hears is a rustle of wind that draws her attention to the towering trees whose knotted branches gesticulate violently and claw the dark sky. The river's rowdy churning makes her look to the bank where bushes quake and night creatures scurry through tall grasses.

Grace trembles and begs, "Rosie, don't leave me!" She calls out, "Where are you?" as a dense blur enters the periphery of her teary vision. Turning to focus on it, she sees that it is a possum stealing toward the river. She gasps reflexively which causes the animal to flinch. And when it stops and turns to face her, Grace registers the horror: Rosie is clamped inside the possum's steely jaw.

"No!" she screams as the possum scampers toward the low brush. Without thinking, she flings her flashlight at it and charges bravely toward it. The flashlight conks the possum's head, stunning the animal, and it turns to face her again, this time baring its spiny yellow teeth. Grace freezes in her tracks and stares helplessly at Rosie who dangles from the possum's black snarling lips. Grieving that she could be losing Rosie forever in this terrible way, she implores, "Please, give her back to me." She cries and points at Rosie, wondering why everything she loves must be taken from her.

The animal scratches the soft earth with its barbed toes and draws back its sinister lips to bare even more of its horrible teeth. Its stink eye glistens scarily. And then, for no apparent reason, it opens its mouth. Rosie drops unceremoniously onto the bank and the possum scuttles away.

"My Rosie!" Grace exclaims as she rushes toward her monkey's tattered body. But when she is mere inches away, a lick of river unfurls onto the bank and drags Rosie into the Baptista. Grace lunges toward her, but her fingers merely brush the new stump of Rosie's arm before Rosie floats away.

Grace rights herself and runs after Rosie who is already tumbling downriver. Calling out Rosie's name, she inches her way downstream along the slippery bank, clutching onto tufts of grass suspended from the inner slope. She finds a tree branch and uses it to fish for Rosie, oblivious to the river encircling her legs above her pink anklets.

Her attempts proving futile, she makes her way to the footbridge where the river has ominously risen to match the height of its span. The bank beyond the bridge is bare of shrubs and grass, preventing her from proceeding farther. Exhausted and bereft, she mounts the bridge and sits down. She clings to one of its posts as the footbridge sways from the impact of the river's choppy currents. She looks dejectedly back upstream, across the strapping ribbons of river that ripple toward her.

Now she cries uncontrollably, thoroughly confused by her overwhelming misery and the senselessness of all her losses. She doesn't understand why so much mysterious sadness must prevail in the world, without fathers and angels and mothers and teachers to explain it. Life, it seems, is just a succession of losses, of having to give up everything you love. Anyone could disappear from the routine of the world without any explanation, and without someone noticing that they were gone.

She cries about Rosie . . . her father's loneliness . . . her mother's lethal sadness. She cries for Tommy's finger and all the ants she killed. She cries about Mrs. Podroski losing her husband . . . Mr. Dunleavy's sickness . . . Miss Maddy's useless legs. She cries for the Rodriguez's baby and all the hungry children in the world . . .

The wind rages, a night owl coos "Who? Who?" and the river washes up against the bridge and splashes her face. Grace shouts into the canyon: "Rosie, come back!" as the lights from Mr. Utley's home extinguish on a faraway hill, the sky turning even darker now.

Grace screams louder and harder until her despair shifts spontaneously into rage. She looks to the heavens and dares its inhabitants, "Go ahead and kill me! I don't care anymore!" She yells so loud that she is deaf to the wind and the river and the agonizing silence of disinterested angels. She screams so hard that she starts to feel faint, and she cannot breathe in without choking on tears. Her body falls limp, and all she wants to do is to sleep forever. She lies down on the footbridge and curls up on her side. And feeling the bridge sway, she is dreamily reminded of rocking high in the sky on the Ferris wheel. Closing her swollen eyes, she re-envisions that night at the carnival, when she and Rosie and her mother and father were pressed into that one happy moment. Her good memory of that night begins to merge with her dreams, and she drifts toward sleep.

But then a bright pink light flashes. It is so intense that it jolts her awake. It floods her vision as it also illuminates the river. She squints, cups her hands over her eyes, and tries to discern the origin of the powerful radiance. And finally, she sees the miracle in her midst: a glorious saving light is beaming from an enormous pink halo that hovers above the Baptista. The beautiful, brilliant "O" blinks in the sky and reflects on the floodwater like luminous cherry lifesavers. And after her vision readjusts to the light, she sees that the halo encircles a human figure. "My angel!" she cries. "You came!"

Yet, almost instantly, the angel disappears and the stark emptiness of the sky returns. It happens so abruptly that Grace wonders whether she hallucinated her angel—whether, like her mother, she sometimes "saw things" that didn't exist.

But then the haloed apparition reappears. Its shiny circle of light flashes again above the hill. Glimmering pink rings toss across the river again. "Please stay with me!" she sobs as thunder shakes the sky, as wind wallops the canyon, and a small orange puff of fur with one glistening eye drifts toward her. "Rosie," she shouts, "I'm here!"

Grace rolls onto her belly and scuttles across the bridge, positioning herself to meet Rosie's oncoming path. But Rosie, who is somersaulting in the onrushing river, suddenly pops out of view. Grace screams and stretches her hands wider. But when Rosie reemerges, she is beyond reach and drifts under the bridge.

Spinning around toward the other side of the bridge, Grace casts her hands blindly into the river. Something enters her grasp, and when she pulls it into view, she is staring into Rosie's scruffy face. "My Rosie!" she cries, holding her tight against her heart, rocking together on the swaying bridge.

The pink halo flashes only weakly now. Grace stands up and looks back toward her fading angel, thanking her for Rosie's return. And, as if in response, the angel raises an open hand to her—a signal to Grace that she and Rosie have been officially saved.

The big pink halo stutters irregularly, and Grace uses its faltering light to retrace her path to the campsite. Once there, she stands on the riverbank and watches the halo extinguish with healing finality.

Grace grabs her father's sleeping bag, and she and Rosie trudge back to her mother's house. Inside the living room, she finds her mother sprawled out on the sofa. There are potato chip crumbs scattered across her chest and splotches of red wine on her T-shirt. Cigarette stench fully claims the air.

After propping Rosie up against a wine tumbler, Grace stands near the couch and listens to her mother's irregular breathing. She loosens the scarf around her mother's neck and repositions her cold dangling arm back onto the couch. Retrieving a blanket from the rocking chair, she drapes it across her mother's limp, rag-doll body. With the damp sleeve of her own shirt, she wipes red wine off her mother's parted mouth.

With Rosie in her arms, she scans the wrecked living room—the overflowing ashtrays, the discarded Stouffer's frozen dinner plates, the withered houseplants, and the empty wine bottles stuffed with worn candles that line the windowsills. Her mother's strange paintings—canvases filled with unrecognizable forms and blurred commotions of colors—are stacked haphazardly everywhere. Paint tubes and pigment-stained brushes are all over the floor.

Grace's renewable sadness refills her. She stares at her mother who does not move, who remains unaware of her presence and the fact of the flood inching toward their home. And she begins to despair as she drifts automatically on a familiar stream of feeling that always courses toward her mother, like an ocean inexorably returning to the same rocky shore.

But something different happens now. Instead, the rage that she discovered tonight on the footbridge washes over and through her. And she pulls back from her mother, like a night tide yanked away by a powerful moon.

She looks at the canvas hanging on her mother's easel. And, like all the others, it is covered with distorted shapes, uneven lines going nowhere, colors randomly arranged. On impulse, she squeezes a tube of black paint into her palm and makes a fist. Then she presses her inky palm against the center of the canvas. When she withdraws her hand, its imprint lingers there—a dark shadow that provides the only recognizable shape on the entire canvas. And she sees how it is uniquely rendered by the whorls of her fingertips, the lines crisscrossing her palm.

She walks to a windowsill and withdraws a wine-bottled candle that she lights with her mother's cigarette lighter. She carries it to the dining room and sets it on the table near her mother's purse. Its flame illuminates several photographs that are thumbtacked to the wall, and she removes one of her mother that she slips into her pocket.

She searches her mother's purse, finally locating an envelope. Before putting that into her pocket, too, she points to its return address and tells Rosie, "It's a letter from dad."

Now she forms a circle with her thumb and index finger above the candle flame, creating a shadowy O that floats on the ceiling. "Look, Rosie," she says, "like our angel's halo tonight."

Then, with Rosie in one hand and the candle in the other, Grace returns to the living room. She tip-toes past her mother and mounts the staircase that leads to her bedroom. Looking back at her mother one last time, she marvels how well she has learned tonight to distinguish so many different shades of darkness.

⌒ saving grace ⌒

"TAKES YOU BACK A FEW DECADES, doesn't it?" says Ella, blowing into her soda straw to create rust-colored bubbles in her root beer.

Norma places her hands on her broad hips, stretches her rounded back, and wearily scans the interior derangement of her beloved tavern. "Sorry, Ella," she says. "I can't go down memory lane and get sentimental with you now. There's too much work left to do here. And besides, I've been trying so hard to let go of the past—my bar, my home, my friends."

Rolling her eyes dismissively, Ella replies, "Olivia's sits on the highest ground for miles. You know it's going to survive this flood."

Norma wipes her palms on her apron. "Oh? And you can guarantee that?"

"I suppose what I mean is that . . . well, it *has* to survive. Olivia's is the heart of our community."

Plopping another hastily packed carton of liquor onto the bar, Norma says, "We both know that floods don't care about such things. They don't have emotions or intentions like we do. They are heartless and impartial exterminators."

Ella sulkily concentrates on rocking her plastic tumbler against the bar counter, watching a watery semi-circle form, listening to the low thrum of plastic against wood. When Norma shoots her a disapproving look, she dabs the watery half-moon with a sleeve of her print smock and complains, "Well, what difference does it make if you're going to ditch this bar?"

"I'm not giving up on Olivia's," Norma says. "I'm just being practical and hedging my bets. If the bar survives the flood, I'll consider reopening it. But if it doesn't—well, that's got to be all right enough because there's nothing you can do about it."

Norma instantly regrets her matter-of-fact tone, realizing it is likely to distress Ella even more. Already Ella's expression—capable of exhibiting infinite injury—registers grievous harm. Moreover, on a practical level, so much sorting and packing remain to secure the bar against flood damage—she doesn't have the time required to mend Ella's feelings. Urgently, she attempts a reparative offering: "Ella, *you* are the heart of Woodhaven. Not this old bar."

"Sure," Ella scoffs. "Maybe the *mouth* of Woodhaven. That's really more like it, isn't it?"

Norma cringes, hearing Ella's tone transition to self-pity—a more daunting emotional tar pit from which to escape. She says, "You're feeling vulnerable now, and insecure. That's all—"

"Hey," Ella interrupts. "I *know* what some people say

behind my back. You don't have to pretend."

"That's nothing but talk," Norma says, filling a Tupperware container with swizzle sticks. "You're the one who keeps people connected around here. The town's always relied on you for that."

"'Connected'? Well, if I'm responsible for *that*, I sure did a great job. Because everyone is *leaving*." Her plastic tumbler thuds against the bar like a judge's gavel.

Norma's patience is waning. She looks out through the tavern's front window on which rain trickles down from the sprawling neon letters that spell out "Olivia's." The gloomy weather reports that continue to broadcast from the AM radio puncture her confidence about having sufficient time to prepare the bar. She blurts out, "Because it's a *flood*, Ella! An act of *God*. People *have* to leave because they could otherwise *drown*."

"Well, you don't have to be sarcastic. This is difficult enough. What I mean is that I'm not hearing about all those 'connected' people planning to return here afterwards."

"Look, I'm sorry," Norma says, regretting her outburst as much for re-injuring Ella's feelings as for further disrupting the progress of their labor. "Besides, you don't know that for sure."

Ella judiciously weighs Norma's apology, trying to decide whether it carries adequate sincerity and regret. Her expression conveys deep deliberation while she trills her fingers against the bar. Finally, sensing that Norma is about to give up on the operative dynamic, she dramatically concedes, "I forgive you."

Frustrated, but willing to settle for a practical peace, Norma exits for therapeutic solitude in the storage room. While passing through its door, she hears Ella mutter: "Ask Juliette if she agrees about me keeping everyone 'connected'."

Rummaging loudly through the supply shelves, Norma tries to generate sufficient commotion to create a protective soundscreen against Ella's deafening self-absorption. Mindlessly nudging Ajax cans and Tide boxes along the shelves, she imagines the exorbitant amount of time she must have spent throughout the years, trying to rearrange her own feelings to accommodate Ella's. Peering through a crack in the doorway, she sees her maddening, self-righteous, egocentric—but generally well-intentioned—friend still sitting at the bar, ostensibly waiting to begin another contentious salvo of self-referential dialogue. But depleted of emotional reserve, Norma cannot surrender to that now. Instead, when she returns to the bar, she looks squarely at Ella and says: "It would have been way too easy for you *without* Juliette. She forced you to think more carefully about the ways in which you genuinely related to people."

Stunned by Norma's directness, Ella replies, "Easy? Nothing's 'easy' about taking responsibility for other people, and at least *trying* to keep them connected. That takes effort, and loads of hard faith. And what in god's name does Juliette have to do with any of that? I don't think she even once gave me the time of day to help me with any of that or—"

"What I mean," Norma says, "is that . . . well, you're a good soul, Ella. You're outwardly kind and generous—almost to a fault. And people here in Woodhaven have always responded to you because of that. Really, how could they not?"

Ella tightens her grasp on the tumbler. "Are you suggesting that what I do for other people and how I relate to them are *gimmicks* to get them to like me? Is that what you're implying?"

Norma gently returns, "Please . . . forget it. Let's not do this now. We're both exhausted, and you're still bruising from how things just ended between you and Juliette."

"Well, you saw how she ignored me. And it hurt— watching the two of you having a drink at the bar without me."

"C'mon, Ella. It was Juliette's last time here. You know we just took a private moment together. Like you and I take all the time, too."

Still, Ella cannot abandon the relational drama to which she is accustomed concerning their threesome. In fact, she is sailing on automatic pilot now, following a fast-moving stream of potent disparagements. Pointing to the center of her chest, she persists, "So, *this* is the real 'heart of the community'? But it is also an *artificial* heart? Do I have that correct?"

"Please," Norma begs. "There's no time—"

"An artificial heart," Ella continues, "so fake that it doesn't give *genuine* life support to our town?"

Norma reminds herself that this is likely the *final* time she will have to endure Ella sitting at the bar, trying so hard to goad her into a murky old dynamic that always leaves each of them sad and befuddled.

"Well, I'm waiting," Ella says, deliberately tightening the tension between them. But then her exquisite radar begins to warn her that Norma might withdraw from the next odd inning between them—and there would be no real victory in that forfeiture.

However, Norma decides to stay in the game. "All right," she says. "I just think—that is, I *believe*—you never appreciated how close you and Juliette actually were. The distance you always rail against—well, it doesn't exist. You see her in a mirror, really. Your yin is her yang—or vice versa. You two are two pieces of one puzzle. Ella, you've never been good at recognizing connections between people when they exist outside of a certain frame."

Ella hisses. "What are you talking about? A 'frame'? What nonsense—"

Norma slaps her hands on the bar. "Calm down! All I'm saying is that you always do favors for people. You take care of them, and you listen to their troubles. You offer advice and answers—even when no one asks for them! You give people all sorts of things. And, so, everyone sees that and appreciates it. And there's nothing wrong with it. But yours is also a way of relating with people that is—well, a very visible way. An obvious way. What you don't understand is that, just like everyone else, you also connect to people in less . . . I don't know . . . less 'nice' ways."

"You mean," says Ella, "like the way you and I are connecting right now?"

Norma throws up her hands in surrender and takes refuge again in the storage room.

Ella's fighting spirit instantly deflates. She cannot believe that Norma walked away, declining to deliver the next pitch. That is not how things are supposed to play out between them, especially during this final inning.

In want of a diversion, Ella walks through the bedraggled bar in search of a distracting task. But she only becomes more agitated, no matter how forcefully she upturns chairs to set them on tables, no matter how vigorously she tosses salt shakers into storage containers.

So, she decides on a self-intervention and sits back down at the bar. After drawing in a few steadying breaths, she vows to adopt a more agreeable mindset. She conjures up the "four tips to positive thinking" that she had learned from a burly psychologist on Oprah's show. She recalls his encouragement to seek self-improvement during times like the present that "overwhelm us with perplexing tension." And she remembers his advisement to "search for the truth behind the veil of one's self-defensiveness." While Norma rummages in the storage room, Ella rummages internally, searching her heart and mind for what onerous personal truths might be operative in her psychic quandaries involving Norma and Juliette.

And yet, after several minutes of serious self-examination, Ella finds no warrant for self-improvement—let alone any evidence of a defensive "veil" she might be wearing. So, she decides to investigate her subconscious even further, focusing on her nemesis, Juliette. She conjures up the same psychologist's "Five Questions to Ask Whenever You Have Troubling Thoughts about Someone." And in quick succession, she answers the first four. But she hesitates on the final question: "In your heart of hearts, could your irritation represent your envy of that person?"

Ella feels the answer before she can articulate it. It arrives as a surge of nausea and makes her feel inadequate of character. "Damn," she whispers, "self-improvement can be so sickening." She also concludes—contrary to the psychologist's guarantee—that "getting down to the truth through earnest self-exploration" does *not* always generate "deep well-being."

But then, she wonders—*If such earnest self-examination leaves me feeling so bad, I must have strayed off the correct self-analytic path.* Surely, to feel so unrewarded must indicate that she'd taken a wrong turn and arrived at an erroneous conclusion. Or perhaps she probed her subconscious too deeply. Indeed, rethinking matters now, no genuinely "apparent" truth should have to require *five* questions for its unearthing.

Regardless of the psychology involved, she realizes that she must concede this troubling admission: She wishes now—as she has wished for decades—that Juliette would simply disappear. It doesn't matter that the flood will effectively grant that wish within a day or two by disbanding each of them to separate cities in California. Because she knows that Juliette is durable beyond mere physical absence, having taken permanent residence in her psyche since the day they met. Already, Ella helplessly imagines her continuing obsession with Juliette after the flood. And she enviously foresees Juliette and Norma maintaining a close friendship that excludes her—meeting regularly for pinochle, taking bus trips to Reno, celebrating each other's birthday.

But the relationships amongst the three of them have never seemed fair, Ella thinks. This, despite her tireless work to maintain the trio's connections, all the while Juliette and Norma took them for granted. Despite her extra effort to forge meaningful bonds with each of them, she never became as close to Norma or Juliette as they became with one another. It makes no rightful sense that she should be the odd one out. Or that she should have to suffer such enigmatic tension with Juliette.

The storage room door bursts open and Norma reappears, unhappily noting the even greater distress evident in Ella's expression. But during her minutes away, she had resigned herself to the fact that, no matter what she did or said, she was going to set off Ella's emotional land mines. And, still, the mission to protect and secure Olivia's had to be prioritized. So, after plunking another box down on the bar, she says, "This one's schnapps," and she hurriedly returns to the storage room.

Ella feels too overwrought to challenge Norma's avoidant behavior. She notes that the afternoon light is dimming fast behind storm clouds, diminishing time and opportunity for further companionship. She counsels herself to fend off the temptation to sulk which will only spoil her final hour with Norma.

Firming her resolve to shift emotional gears, she places her palms on the bar, feeling its solidity, hoping for the return of her own. She runs her fingers across its sleek redwood, tracing initials that patrons have carved into it. She touches the bar's dedication plate that bears Tomasz Podroski's name, and suddenly, too suddenly, she feels the excruciatingly real and tangible end to her life in Woodhaven.

Norma's provocative comments return to her consciousness, igniting uncomfortable self-incrimination about her failure to create a lasting sense of community to draw people back after the flood. Is it conceivable, she dares now bleakly wonder, that she is actually blameworthy for the diaspora? Is Norma correct about a grand false performance that she delivers which others experience as inauthentic? In fact, might that also be the basis for all her interpersonal failures, and with people other than Juliette? Like Olivia, slipping out of town one day without even saying goodbye. Her own sons moving to such faraway colleges on the eastern seaboard. Patsy's parents shunning her advice about accepting their daughter's baby. Maddy consistently declining offers of her assistance and accompaniment to social events. Bill routinely rejecting her efforts to save him from self-destruction. Trina refusing to speak with her after she offered to help with raising Grace.

How have so many people so vigorously rejected my offers of kinship?

She struggles to contain her heart's dispiriting commotion, an exponentially more daunting task as she scans the bar and witnesses upheaval everywhere. The exterior disarray only aggravates her interior calamity. Chairs upside down. The "Olivia's" sign sprawled backwards across the window. Liquor crates all over the pool table. Storage bags on windowsills. Lamps lying on their sides.

When Norma reenters with an armful of dusty bourbon bottles, Ella calmly asks, "Do *you* think anyone will return after the flood?"

Taken aback by Ella's display of vulnerability, Norma pauses. "Well," she says finally, "I think it depends. Some people, like Maddy or Ed, may have to come back—*if* their places survive. Their needs have been so particularly met here, I can't imagine them starting up somewhere new. Can you?"

"I suppose not," Ella says, further wounded by Norma not committing to her own return.

"But the young ones?" Norma continues. "With time and money to reinvent their lives, I don't see them returning. They have more options to create new communities, or move to more exciting cities. And with all their social networking, they can relocate anywhere and still stay in touch with each other."

Ambling toward the stereo speakers at the rear of the bar, Ella wearily concedes, "I suppose that's how it is nowadays. Still, I have to ask—since when did mobility and 'virtual' communities become so important to people? Why doesn't it matter anymore to stay put in real life, with stable roots, in a flesh-and-blood community with actual people?"

"That era passed long ago," says Norma. "Even in this town, nothing's been the same since they closed the factory during the War. Our community's been in constant flux. But that's the natural order."

Ella searches Norma's expression, hoping to detect a trace of uncertainty. There being none to witness, she admits, privately, that Norma is right. The world keeps spinning, nations constantly reform, entire species disappear every day, a spacecraft recently sailed beyond Mars, a black president occupied the White House, and spinal cords were growing in Petri dishes. She responds with manufactured cheerfulness, "Of course, you're right." Then she dutifully carries the schnapps box to the pool table and stacks it alongside crates that read: "Gin," "Whiskey," "Wine—Red," or "Wine—White."

Norma says, "And it's just a matter of time before the millennials discover Woodhaven. After this flood, the land and any remaining homes will become even less expensive. Besides, Woodhaven's a great place for the 'green living' movement. You watch. They'll renovate what remains, convert our farms into organic gardens, start wireless-ready B&B's, and establish 'cuisine' restaurants. Woodhaven will still exist, Ella, but it will be a very different Woodhaven. It won't look anything like the current one."

"I don't think I'd want to live in a community that didn't care about anything or anyone preceding it," Ella says. "Unique human histories were lived out here— meaningful, substantial ones. And together they created a story of Woodhaven that's worth remembering and retelling."

Norma sighs. "Well, the flood has already erased much of that history. Our museum's gone. The elementary school is destroyed. The fields are ruined, and our commercial center is under water. I doubt that any home in the midcanyon is going to survive. And we can't do anything about any of that. Really, Ella, it's our time to let go. We must accept—as graciously as possible—that a new history is going to be written here. A history that won't include us."

Despite her own advice, Norma feels acutely depressed as she registers the emotional weight of the losses she has just articulated. Then she considers her old friend and suddenly feels foolish for having spent these final moments in Olivia's, trying to preserve *things* like plates and bottles, bowls and wineglasses. In a turnabout celebratory gesture, she says, "Ella, we're through here! Now it's come hell or high water what's left of this place." Heading outside to the storage shed, she declares, "I'm getting that Dom Perignon for us!"

Ella happily sets down the stack of CDs that she'd been sorting and calls after Norma, "Be careful! It's getting dark out there! And the electricity's finicky."

The prospect of sharing *the* Dom Perignon with Norma warms Ella instantly. The keepsake bottle from the bar's christening nearly sixty-five years ago had been gifted to Norma when Olivia handed over the bar to her. Tonight, a rich and complex history of the bar would be savored by two of the town's few residents who remember—both that and why—the bottle even exists.

Waiting for Norma to retrieve the champagne, Ella looks to the high shelves along the tavern walls. They

teem with sports trophies and gewgaws that com-
memorate multigenerational victories in bar-
sponsored tractor pulls, bowling leagues, spelling bees,
and, more recently, soccer tournaments. They display
dozens of souvenir shot glasses from countries visited
by local residents. Encased in a glass cabinet are five
clocks created in 1950 by Woodhaven elementary classes to mark the half-century. They are heavily deco-
rated—with shellacked candy corn, macaroni noodles,
pink seashells, dappled glitter, and glued-on 1950 copper pennies—reminding Ella how time could look so
shiny and recreational to the young. Three of the
clocks had ceased working long ago, each frozen in a
unique moment. The remaining two kept discordant
times, providing Norma with a choice each night: to
close the bar either a little early or a little late.

Anticipating her final drink here tonight with Norma, Ella realizes how much she's going to miss their
shared after-hours rituals at Olivia's. For years, she
has often helped Norma close the bar at night, ending the
evening by sipping rum-and-Cokes at the window table.
They would talk as they stared out at the moonlit hills
and canyon, watching the pink neon light from the
"Olivia's" sign alighting on the Baptista like fluttery
ribbons.

Determined to enjoy this last evening together, Ella
sets out to locate festive paper umbrellas to embellish
their champagne glasses. She searches the drawers
under the sink, sorting through rainbow-colored soda
straws, thumbtacks, leprechaun-bearing swizzle
sticks, and trick ice cubes containing rubber eyeballs
or spiders. Behind variously worn wax candles and
assorted cake decorations, she comes across a yel-

lowed index card bearing the hand-written details of Annie Podroski's prize-winning canapé recipe.

Underneath the card is an old photograph on which is written: "Olivia's, Opening Day—March 6, 1944." Ella withdraws her reading glasses from the pocket of her print smock and studies the photograph under the erratic lights that are marginally powered by the failing electrical supply. She sees Olivia—so youthful and strong—standing in front of the bar, gleefully upholding *the* Dom Perignon to the camera. She is surrounded by women in dresses who lift beer mugs—and they look directly into the camera and directly through time, to the very moment from which Ella looks back at them now. In the background are sturdy young men—some in uniform. Bill Dunleavy's parents stand with Maddy's, and their foursome looks like a giddy chorus line. Annie Podroski holds a small wooden doll and sits on a blanket with her parents and Tomasz.

Ella dries her eyes and slips the photograph into her pocket. Composing herself, she squares her smock across her shoulders and pats down her gray flyaway hair. She dims the sputtering ceiling lights to conserve what electricity remains, and then she walks to the window overlooking the canyon. She thinks about how often she has stood here before, watching the seasons inexorably cycle, the Baptista zigzagging through the valley. She remembers spotting Trina Woods once, behind a sagebrush, trysting with a stranger. Raj Joshipura scribbling in a notebook. Annie and Tomasz picnicking on a checkered tablecloth. Doc McCracken sobbing on the footbridge. Nick Archer playing saxophone on a hillside.

Staring at the bloated Baptista illuminated by a timid moon, she envisages herself fading from the lives of her friends and neighbors. Within the week, the flood will erase her community, annihilate its buildings, demolish its farms, even reshape its hills and canyon. Nothing familiar will remain. Having always depended upon a landscape of other people to define herself, she wonders how she will be remembered, or if she'll be remembered at all.

The door creaks open. Norma sets the champagne on the bar and says, "Hey! I can't see anything in here."

"Bring the bottle over here," Ella calls out. "Let's take our drinks at the window table one last time."

"Sure," Norma says, making her way. "Like old times. So, we might as well turn on the sign, too—what's left of it anyway."

While Norma sets the table and rights its chairs, Ella walks to an electrical socket and plugs in the power cord to light up the front window sign. Damaged by the storms, only the sign's huge "O" remains defiantly operative.

Tonight, Ella and Norma watch the creamy pink neon circulate through the "O" like luminous blood. The "O" pulses while the electricity stutters, tossing incandescent rings into the bar and out through the window. Waiting for Norma to pop the cork, Ella takes in her final views of the river and canyon. Her face and neck warm from the rosy glow of the big "O" through which she peers.

Now the waning electricity sputters, the "O" flickers on and off, and Ella sees the canyon illuminate like a series of snapshots. She presses her palm against the window, as though touching a picture of her life with finality. "Goodbye," she whispers as Norma pops the cork, the refrigerator silences, two clocks tick asymmetrically, and the neon "O" frazzles and yields to darkness.

⌒ high school reunion ⌒

AT LEAST IT REQUIRED an act of biblical proportions to deliver me here, Jake tells himself as he looks around and appraises the high school evacuation center where he is supposed to feel "safe" now.

But it has been raining for weeks, and already he feels partially dissolved within the watery world that has been absorbing more of him each day. His skin and muscles feel like saturated sponge. The dense pewter sky weighs so heavily on his skull that he cannot separate his thoughts from the encroaching rains. In his dreams, his watery interior merges with the floodwaters that have seeped into his home, covered his floors, risen steadily under his bed. Last night, he dreamt that his spleen and liver drifted out of his abdomen and traveled with currents of the Baptista, trailing the beer cans that sailed off his porch the day before.

The high school grounds teem with befuddled exiles who clutch bottles of drinking water and bulky garbage bags. They shift aimlessly, continuously, on this high ground, drifting back and forth and back again. The air is a continuously drizzling sea. Children splash one another in rain puddles while their parents watch indifferently. He hears the bloated Baptista rumble beneath the commotion of these dismantled lives, sees it pushing against the tenuous boundaries of this so-called safety zone.

"You'll be fine once we get you to the high school," Sheriff Strather promised an hour before. "The Red Cross has been setting up shelter all night."

Jake remembers hanging mid-air onto the Sheriff's words, with one foot in the rescue boat and the other planted on the roof of his canyon rental. He pictures himself then—legs extended, arms flailing—like a spastic starfish teetering above a watery abyss. He recalls in that moment his great hesitation about being saved, about being delivered to purported shelter here at his dreaded alma mater. But he yielded haplessly to the arc of his body's trajectory—through space, off the roof, over the choppy river, into the Sheriff's wet arms.

More than three decades have passed since he last visited Woodhaven High. And now, from his position on the school's muddy lawn, a few steps beyond the Sheriff's boat, he wonders if the school has tripled in size. Its main entry, an unilluminated portal through which people stream, looks like a dark, hungry mouth.

"Hey, buddy," the Sheriff calls.

Jake looks back, peering over the low-set visor of his cap to see the Sheriff's worried face. "Go on inside," he instructs, "with all the others there."

Jake raises his thumb to indicate compliance. Still, turning back and shuffling toward the school, he mutters, "God help me."

To keep the gymnasium out of view, he lowers his head while he walks to a bench. He sits alongside an elderly woman who is wrapped in a blanket and who stares ahead, without vision, into the courtyard of displaced people. He removes his backpack and sets it on wet pavement between his muddied brown boots. Breathing forcibly into his chest, he tries to quell his anxiety and reassure himself that he will survive this place of false refuge.

Still, his private panic does not recede. In fact, it expands as he soaks up more of the public panic surrounding him. The frenzied volunteers tossing sandbags to one another are moving like a frantic caterpillar along the high school's borders. Then, the despairing bent women, clutching their foreheads. The confused old men displaced from the veterans' home. The anxious wet-haired children who search their parents' worried faces for answers.

Jake idly watches rain stream down a fold in his raincoat sleeve and drip onto the pavement. And he thinks about how he has always measured his life in terms of distance from this place. Thirteen years ago, traveling through Riyadh in the rumbling back seat of a military van, he did the math with a blue ink pen against his khakis, figuring his position—7,312 miles southeast of Woodhaven. Throughout his career as an accountant, he routinely estimated the miles of separation between the business conventions he attended and this town where he grew up. Three months ago, after his company declared bankruptcy and laid him off, he moved back to Woodhaven to help his mother transition into the convalescent home in Glen Cove. He rented a garage apartment in Thalburg Canyon that was, by his calculation, two and one-quarter miles east of the high school.

Rubbing his chafed legs, he stares at his boots that twitchily tap the pavement. He swallows several times, trying to quench the parched column of his throat, while looking wistfully at people who carry bottled water as they mill about. They all seem so tribal and far away. He smiles forcefully, in a mechanical sort of way, hoping that someone will welcome him into the communal drama. But they all just drift by, moving seamlessly amongst each other like waves, directed by natural forces that do not include him.

The massive iron bell in the high school tower rings. Its dull metallic reverberation is so exquisitely familiar that it simply bypasses all his usual defenses. Its triggering sound lands directly in the clenched fold of his brain that has held his memories of Woodhaven High in such tight seclusion. The fold opens and unleashes all it has tried to suppress. There is Patsy's freckled face, and the minty scent of her shampoo. The scuff of her high-heeled boots across the gymnasium floor . . .

Jake starts humming, desperate to externalize something of himself so that he does not completely implode. But then a man's intrusive voice falters through the public speakers: "Attention, everyone! The Red Cross is serving sandwiches and snacks in the gymnasium."

Gymnasium. That awful word. It travels the path newly forged by the tower bell, arriving like a missile in the same clenched fold, dislodging even more buried memories. Now, the taste of Patsy's cherry lipstick when they kissed . . . Patsy crying . . . a metal door slamming. He tries to resist the sickening pull of his past, but then the tower bell tolls again, and he falls back in time, loses all distance between "now" and "then." He plummets through layers of his past until he arrives at the moment that he has tried so hard to forget. And, forced to examine it now . . . he is stunned to see how faithfully it has been preserved. The world of that moment, trapped in amber—April 26, 1977. He is standing in front of Patsy who sits cross-legged on the gymnasium floor, wearing his varsity jacket over her waffle vest. She is looking directly up at him, her full lips downturned. Her hazel eyes glisten beneath her lilac eye shadow, and tears loiter on the tip of her freckled nose. Her black hair sweeps her shoulders, and a ridge shows where her headband usually rests. She wears a white blouse with a straight collar, and a denim skirt that drapes over the new growth in her belly. Her left hand bears the varsity ring he gave her six months earlier.

"Holy shit," is all he says when she tells him that she is pregnant.

Patsy cringes. And when she can finally speak, she manages, "What are we going to do?" She buries her face in her hands.

But Jake hears "we" as though it were a foreign word. He feels unrelated to the emotional scene unfolding before him. He glances at the window behind Patsy, and he sees them both reflected in its glass. In the reflection, he stands tall and handsome in his favorite sweatshirt with its torn-off sleeves. His young biceps bulge without effort, and thick finger-combs streak his slicked-back coppery hair. The fluorescent ceiling light falls on his angular face to create a dramatic shadowy effect which highlights a jagged scar across one of his cheekbones. He sees the back of Patsy's lowered head reflected in the bottom of the pane.

Then he looks directly at his reflection, directly into his own eyes. And in a private moment fully detached from the rest of the world, he sees himself in a flattering light—strong and expansive, endowed with new power and potential. He even imagines his potent reflection casting out through the window, stretching far beyond Woodhaven High. He experiences a wild rush, and he smiles at himself in the window. It is a fleeting, reflexive, self-congratulatory smile meant only for him.

He is oblivious to Patsy's movement. But in that moment, she abruptly turns her head and looks up, in time to catch him smiling. She gasps and, like a lightning bolt to his eyes, her wounded expression enters his awareness.

THIS WHIPLASH OF MEMORY fills him with self-loathing and causes him to flinch. The elderly woman sitting beside him places a comforting hand on his arm, and she studies him with obvious concern. But he cannot tolerate her kindness while so shamefully aware of his reprehensible behavior. He smiles feebly at her before collecting his backpack and walking away.

There is no escape, he thinks. *I'm standing here at ground zero. I cannot create any saving distance now.*

He braces himself before crossing the school lawn. And finally, he stands directly outside the old gymnasium window. Looking into its reflection now, more than three decades later, he sees a balding, pear-shaped man standing in the mud.

He closes his eyes and surrenders fully to the old defining moment, inviting his clenched memory to release fully at last. As it opens further, there is Patsy's wounded gaze searching his expression for any evidence of his love or concern. But his awkward heart can't bear her astonishment, and he only turns away in a reflex born of panic and disgrace. Before he can gather the wherewithal to explain his stupid behavior, she is hurrying away, her boots scuffing across the basketball court, the tower bell ringing, the gymnasium door slamming.

THUNDER RATTLES THE SKY and returns Jake to the present, to the children screaming in the soccer field, to a rescue helicopter sputtering overhead. He wishes he could see Patsy again and ask for her forgiveness. He needs to believe that her life has not remained tethered to his crass moment of primitive bravado. He prays that she has been freed from his cruelty and able to look into other men's eyes. And he wants her to see him, too—the person he is now—so that he will not feel forever reflected by her wounded look.

He returns to the courtyard and resurveys the crowd. People swarm around the Red Cross van, warming their hands around steaming coffee cups. He spots a burly man in a yellow slicker who stands alone at a sandwall beyond the soccer field. A playful young couple on the gymnasium steps gesture broadly to one another—their arms reach to the sky, the man falls to his knees, the woman pretends to swoon—and they kiss. A girl wearing pink boots thrusts a tattered orange monkey with a single eye into her father's hands, and he masterfully wrings out the monkey's three sodden limbs.

Jake wonders what happened to Patsy and the baby. Whether Patsy ever graduated. Whether her disowning parents ever reclaimed her. Whether she has ever thought about him kindly. Mostly, he wonders about their child, the child who frequents his dreams.

He steps gingerly into the crowd, transfixed by the father who now returns the orange monkey to his daughter. She cautiously appraises her monkey's strangeness, but is instantly relieved when she looks back to her father whose tender expression brims with conviction.

Jake painfully envisions his own child searching for him, bearing a wound that only he can fix. And he wishes he could look back into his child's eyes—his now thirty-some-year-old child's eyes—with that father's same reassuring look.

He maneuvers to the center of the courtyard. People drift by on their mysterious currents. He tries to steady himself by anchoring his attention on one person at a time. A silver haired woman gamely chasing a boy who runs through chains of rain puddles. A middle-aged man leaning against a tree, clutching a blue envelope and staring at the sky. A woman with a polka-dot umbrella who tries to beckon the lone man at the sandwall.

And when he looks to a woman with gray flyaway hair, she turns and catches his gaze. She stands still in her print smock that rustles in the breeze, and for a brief eternity they hold each other's gaze. They keep silent company as the rain continues to fall, the world continues to spin, and time unfolds in its unpredictable pace.

⌒ you get the picture ⌒

YES, YES, YES. I HAD SEX with Bill Dunleavy in a carnival tent last year. Do I regret it? Well, you tell me if I should.

But first, look around my house—at all my art. See?

Now, I may not be the most talented painter in the world. But I have created pieces that galleries in L.A. or New York could show without shame.

Still, no one in Woodhaven gets that. *No one.*

People here look at my paintings, and—I swear to god—if they don't see a kitty, or some damn bowl of fruit, or a sailboat on the river—well, they think my work has no value whatsoever.

Hell, you couldn't sell a decent painting in this town without attaching it to a coupon for a bucket of Kentucky Fried or a six-pack.

So—me having sex with Bill? *That* turned out to be my greatest creative achievement in Woodhaven. It made everyone *respond*. It stirred their passions and curiosity. It inspired their wonder. It made them imagine their own capacity to act outside the old frameworks of their little lives.

And all of that was my doing. My urges, my conceptual powers, my artistic sensibilities created that picture for them.

Real art—like this angry flood pounding at my door—always involves danger and destruction to create something new.

So, please—go ahead. Tell me if you think I should have regrets about Bill.

at redemption's edge

THE RODRIGUEZ FAMILY'S MUD-CAKED TRUCK
swerves across the rain-slicked highway and bumps
off a roadside barrier. Rosa is driving, and her husband Carlos sits beside her. Their three children—
Baby Christina and the eight-year-old twins, Leo and
Maria—sit in the cramped back seat of the extended
cab. Their collective gasp nearly drowns out the tire
squeals as the truck rights on the road.

Outside, on the attached flatbed that is stacked
with the family's possessions, is Buddy—their
three-legged greyhound. He slides treacherously between all the bungeed-down furniture and crates, and
his paws tap frenetically every time the truck swerves.

Occasionally, he lunges against the flatbed sidewalls or the cab's back window.

It is the family's final exit from their rambling farmhouse that straddles the outskirts of the Dunleavy's expansive property. By nightfall, they will begin their new lives in a two-room apartment on the ninth floor of a high-rise complex in Fresno.

The local news plays continuously on the unreliable radio, delivering relentlessly repetitive reports about incessant rain, floodwaters rising, endangered livestock, families fleeing, lives in ruin. As Rosa maneuvers the truck around yet another felled utility pole, a frantic newscaster announces that the Sheriff's helicopter was urgently summoned from the lower canyon where its crew had been laboring to airlift a cow stranded on the Archer family's rooftop. He breathlessly reports, "It's heading," to midcanyon, where a woman has been spotted in the Baptista, clinging to a blue raft . . ."

"My God," Rosa exclaims, gripping the steering wheel harder as the truck bounces over more fallen branches and rogue stones. "I wonder who—"

"Stay calm," Carlos says. "Let's focus on getting to Fresno in one piece."

"I am calm!" she shoots back. "Stop trying to drive!"

"All I'm saying is—"

"You're making me nervous, Carlos! I don't need that right now."

During the silent truce that follows, the radio signal falters. News reportage becomes spotty and telegraphic, the announcer's voice hopping-skipping-and-jumping over details about the flood, the rescuers, the dazed cow, the drowning woman. Leo kicks the backseat speaker, but still they only hear: ". . . the midcanyon completely flooded . . . more National Guardsmen being called in . . . gusts of 68 miles per hour recorded in the East Ridge hills . . . to assist evacuations . . . the identity of the woman in the river withheld until . . . toxic backup from sewage lines . . ."

"Do we have to keep listening to this?" Maria complains. "It's hurting my ears."

Carlos turns to convey a telling look that advises her silence. He also glances at Leo, noting how responsibly he holds Baby Christina, and a wave of admiration courses through him.

"But, Dad," Maria says, "it's the *same* news over and over! We can fill in the blanks. 'More rain. More flood. More rain and flood.' Please—let's take a break."

Rosa shouts, "No! I need to hear about the road conditions. So, everyone be quiet! And don't wake Christina."

"Come on," Maria persists. "Just a little music for one minute?"

Rosa slaps her palm on the dashboard, knocking over a plastic statue of St. Christopher. Her clenched expression signals to Carlos that she has exceeded the limit of her patience. Additional disturbance will only risk the drive.

"Okay, everyone," Carlos intervenes, "we're going to compromise." He clears his throat and begins to sing: "Old man river, that old man river, he just keeps moving—"

"Stop, dad," Maria interrupts. "I mean real music. *Good* music."

Carlos pretends offense. "I can sing. May I remind you that I used to sing with *su abuelo* in a band when we all lived—"

A squall pitches sheets of rain against the truck, creating watery cascades across the windows.

"Look!" says Rosa. "It's hard enough paying attention to this awful road so we're not all killed. Everyone, shut up!"

For a long while, only the newscaster's scratchy reports punctuate the family's silence: "Earlier sightings of horses in the highway . . . all power is now out in the north canyon . . . guardsmen still trying to evacuate a few stragglers . . . expected to reach flood stage within the next two to three . . ."

Carlos slumps into his seat. He idly examines his calloused hands, noting the permanent soil moons underneath his fingernails. It makes him think about the fields he is leaving behind that hold his family's history, and, of course, the coffin of his firstborn.

The truck skids sideways on a slick sheet of rain. One tire loses traction and another bounces over a pothole that sprays water like a fountain. Rosa screams "No!" as she slams the brakes and struggles to correct their course. Carlos braces his hands against the dashboard as he also checks his children's safety in the back. He sees Maria sitting rigidly, and

Leo clutching Christina to his chest—his eyes wide open and his mouth forming an "O".

After the truck steadies, Carlos says, "Let me drive now."

But Rosa seethes, "It's not my fault! It's the *road!* In case you haven't noticed, we're driving through a—"

"Hey!" Carlos says, "it's just that you've been up all night. And maybe you're—"

"None of that changes the *road!*"

Resignedly, he throws up his hands. *Anything to keep her calm.* He turns up the radio volume as the newscaster exclaims, ". . . unbelievable, really! We're flying over the East Ridge hills . . . homes and other buildings look dwarfed in the flood . . . an upturned tractor blocking entrance to . . . so many chickens perched on fences . . . another roof sailing down the Baptista . . ."

Carlos listens to the reporter's fevered descriptions of Woodhaven's dissolution. They sound remote and off-target, oddly referenced to streets and buildings, to businesses and bridges, to things composed of concrete and steel. But the Woodhaven he knows is defined by orchards and vineyards, canyon and river. Its geography is mapped by the labor of his hands and those of his family's before.

He silently prays that his twins will remember the Baptista as something other than the destructive force it has newly become. He resolves to keep them reminded about the river's past benevolence and beauty, and to request that they keep the river's history alive. He will retell how the Baptista nourished the *abierto fru-*

tilla that sprang from the land their ancestors tilled. He'll describe how uniquely sweet were the tomatoes that his grandfather cultivated before industrial farmers took over with toxic chemicals and mechanical fruit pickers. He will tell them about the juiciest strawberries in all of California that seasonally erupted on their family's land at the mouth of the river. He'll recount for them how the river's arms reached into the canyon to irrigate his father's peach and apple orchards that were later lost to the Dunleavys' greater fortunes. He'll show them a photograph of his aunt who lived in a riverbank camper and held the power to speak to the vines. And he will tell of land on the West Ridge hillside that his mother privately claimed with her clandestine planting of lavender, jasmine, and wildflowers.

His heart clenches as their truck approaches the exit sign marking Woodhaven's southernmost boundary. It reads, "Thank you for visiting Woodhaven! The *Original* Home of Thalburg Gelatin." The weather-beaten sign triggers his recall of his grandfather's alternate perspective: "Home of the Thalburg *Curse*." And he imagines his grandfather divining karmic retribution in the occasion of this flood.

By his grandfather's account, the Thalburg Gelatin factory killed the Rodriguez family's way of life. It destroyed their traditions and upended the values that they carried to America on their backs. When the factory's doors opened, family members dropped their shovels and spades and cutters in the fields. They flocked to the Thalburg production lines, lured by offers of steady wages and health insurance. Hands once attuned to a natural rhythm while turning earth for ripe berries began, instead, to turn in repetitive, mechanical ways to process artificially sweetened fruit-flavored gelatin powders.

Carlos recalls his own guilt and relief once his grandfather finally surrendered to the dominion of "the curse." Because it had occurred just in time—just before Rosa arrived from Mexico and flatly rejected the fields for a cashier's job at Markowicz's Food Mart.

Now, looking sidelong at Rosa, Carlos remembers how handsome she looked when she arrived from Oaxaca. How eagerly she began her American life in Woodhaven, first learning English with Ella's help by studying grocery ads in the *Woodhaven Courier*: "Cheerios" and "Pop-Tarts" and "vitamin-fortified milk" . . .

He thinks, *And now, all the words we have between us, in Spanish and English—how inadequate they are to name what we leave behind today.* He digs his soiled fingernails into his thighs, wondering if his firstborn's headstone will resist dislodgment from the flood-saturated ground.

As always, whenever he is reminded of his dead baby, his obsessive questioning begins. Did she cry out that awful afternoon? Did he somehow not hear her helpless plea? Had he been too distracted by the ball-game on television? Was he daydreaming while the nightmare unfolded? And, in the end, still—how does any child die without some stirring cue to their father's heart? How had he heard nothing and felt nothing while she lay dying a stone's throw away in her crib?

He drives his fingernails deeper into his flesh, remembering Rosa's return home that afternoon. She was wearing her red cashier's uniform emblazoned with "MFM" across the front. He can still hear the one-two drop of her white loafers on the hallway floor as he lay half-awake on the sofa. He remembers being roused by her kiss on his forehead before she headed straight to the baby's room. And then the foreboding silence when he switched off the TV—so short, and, yet, so intense an interval—before Rosa's heart-stopping screams began.

It had taken only minutes for Doctor McCracken to arrive. "Crib death," he confidently declared, and "crib death" he kept repeating all the while that Rosa wailed.

Carlos remembers how, in the days and weeks that followed, he kept repeating the doctor's words to Rosa and, privately, to himself. But she kept blaming the toxic fields, the chemicals from crop dusters, her own foolishness for leaving Oaxaca in the first place. She blamed the poisonous river she had to cross under cover of darkness to reach Texas while pregnant with their baby—its sinister waters hexed by the blood of thousands who had failed the crossing.

He peers through the rain-streaked windshield, to the watery road leading them away from their family's past. It is unbearable, leaving his baby behind. He is haunted now by images of her small coffin loosening from the rain-soaked ground, rising up through liquefying earth. He wonders if Rosa is also worrying about that, and whether she will be the one to break their long pact of silence about the baby.

The brakes screech. Buddy slams against the cab's back window and barks uncontrollably. The truck swerves and bounces against an embankment. Carlos yells, "Leo, hang on to Christina!" Maria screams, Leo clutches Christina to his chest, and Rosa pumps the brake while shouting, "Damn!"

The truck shimmies across the road, Leo shields Christina with his body, and Carlos tries to grab the steering wheel. The truck spins around once, twice, three times, and then it slides sideways across the road. Its momentum sends it crashing through the guardrail, skidding over roadside gravel, and heading toward a cliff. Storage crates fling off the flatbed.

Amidst the grievous calamity of his family's screams and, pinned against the door, Carlos reaches for his wife and children at once. Acid roils inside his stomach and scorches his throat as the truck hurdles over a boulder. His memory flashes on the lifeless bodies floating on the moonlit river that he crossed to America. The truck lurches to an abrupt stop at the edge of a hillside pass, and, looking out through the cracked windshield, Carlos sees a front tire that spins free of the ground, dark formless clouds beneath it. The truck engine idles, blood pounds against his skull, Rosa moans, Maria sobs, and Leo slumps in his seat as Christina rolls from his lap and drops to the floor.

"Don't move!" Carlos yells as the truck teeters precariously at the cliff's edge. But Buddy runs agitatedly back and forth on the flatbed, flailing against its jostled cargo of chairs and tables and mattresses. The truck rocks hazardously, and Carlos begs everyone to keep calm. "Sit, Buddy! Sit!" he yells through the blown-out passenger window. But Buddy repeatedly flings himself against cabin, barking hysterically, while the children scream.

"Quiet!" Rosa pleads while tracking Buddy's movements through the rear-view mirror. But her plea is as much an attempt to silence her own menacing thoughts that keep telling her what she must do. Staring blankly at Carlos, she reaches under the seat while the truck continues to jostle from Buddy's continued frenzy.

But Carlos intervenes. He unfastens his safety belt that now cuts into his chest, and he pushes aside Rosa's hand. He takes control of the handgun and of the mutual decision they have arrived at wordlessly. He privately vows, *I will not lose another child.* Then he cocks the trigger and maneuvers the gun through the broken window, aiming at Buddy and shooting.

The gunshot echoes throughout the canyon. Buddy's bark silences, and his endangering movements cease. The sea-saw creaking of the truck's suspension quiets down. Carlos withdraws his arm and drops the gun into his lap.

Looking through the rear-view mirror, Rosa no longer sees Buddy. But she sees the twins frozen in fear, Christina in Leo's lap. And, staring at them all, she is reminded of her lost child, visualizing her as she might appear now—eleven years old, sitting with the others in the back seat. And to her great astonishment, she imagines her daughter looking back, conveying that she is not troubled with her mother's same doubts.

But then Buddy springs back into her view. He leaps off the flatbed, unbalancing the truck again, tipping it further over a cliff. The children panic, their screams are deafening, and the truck begins its swift descent down a steep hill. Carlos tries to touch his children one final time, to assure them of his presence, to let them know they are not alone.

The truck stammers several yards before it flips over, flinging everyone downside, tossing Christina to Maria's feet, and halting finally at a tilt midway down the hillside.

Maria pulls Christina to her lap, trying not to rock the truck, but no one otherwise moves or speaks. The truck dangles perilously and makes strange, hissing noises. Maria whimpers, "Christina's not moving."

Carlos carefully reaches for Christina while also trying to counterbalance his weight against gravity's pull on the truck. But Christina's body suddenly rigidifies in Maria's arms, her plump arms and mottled legs extend fiercely, her neck bends back, her eyes roll up, her face turns blue; she jerks wildly in Maria's lap, and the truck begins to pitch ominously. Carlos tries to counter the physical disturbances created by Christina's seizing, but he cannot accurately anticipate her body's irregular fits. The truck rocks and creaks, teetering, absorbing the violent thrusts of his child's thrashing body. A harsh clanging noise sounds from the truck, and its front hood pops open to emit ghostly smoke.

Rosa sits dazed, paralyzed by the prospect of losing all her children, ashamed of the horrible calculation she keeps computing in her head: *that the twins might be saved if Christina . . .*

She does not respond when Carlos calls her name. Already she is withdrawing from the world, from an unthinkable horrific choice made thinkable. She braces for the abyss, ridding herself of all feeling, deadening her heart.

Carlos recognizes his wife's retreat into benumbing despair. Already she has withdrawn from any deliberation and left him alone with the decision that need be made.

He steels his heart. He tells himself to become a machine. He forces himself to look away from his wife and the twins, and to focus on what he must do. And he makes the same horrible calculation once, twice— the conclusion remaining the same. So he reaches for Christina, with cold rational calculus guiding his earth-stained hands. They approach Christina's clenched mouth from which harsh guttural sounds emerge while her body flails violently, and while Leo weeps, Maria turns away, Rosa faints, the truck slides further downhill.

But when his hand alights on Christina's lips, he hears at last the dying cry of his firstborn child. He hears it dislodge finally from her small throat, rise from her crib, and enter the present inconceivable moment. Reflexively, his hands withdraw from the horror they were about to create. They reach instead for Leo and Maria, as Christina's seizing intensifies, as the truck continues its downhill descent.

Everyone screams and holds on to one another as the truck plunges headfirst, catapulting boxes and lamps and tables into the sky, slamming against the hillside, rolling over, somersaulting, losing all contact with the ground, free-falling free-falling free-falling downward, crashing through hillside pines. A deep boom sounds when the truck plunges into the swollen ravine.

Carlos grabs Christina and hoists her above the floodwater that rises swiftly inside the truck. He holds her face up against the roof as the layer of air rapidly thins. Leo escapes through the shattered back window, pulling Maria with him. Carlos uses his legs to push Rosa out of the truck, her body scraping against glass as she floats away.

Now the water rises to his chin, and he inhales deeply. He presses his lips around Christina's mouth and nose, and he breathes into her as the water envelops them. He holds her like this as he struggles to swim free of the truck, one life breathing deeply for the other's. Seconds later, as swiftly as the flash flood had arrived, it begins to recede, leaving Carlos standing in the ebbing floodwaters, cradling his crying child.

$\smile$ deliverance $\smile$

SAINT THERESA RUMBA'D and, in apparent ecstasy, somersaulted off the refrigerator and plunged into the germander pot below. The perennial nativity scene—its baby Jesus long absent—rocked wildly atop the television set, and its miniature ceramic sheep trailed off to their watery demise below. Saint Thomas wobbled precariously and tackled Saint Joseph on a bookshelf. The crucifix trembled against the wall, and stacks of holy cards on the stereo cabinet toppled like dominoes. Votive candles that suspended from agitated ceiling chains swung free of their flames, leaving only a tired moonlight to illuminate Ed Utley's seismically vibrating living room.

He struggled to rise from the recliner in which he had fallen asleep. And when he stood, his cane slipped from his ancient unsteady hand and dropped into the quivering floodwater. He tried to catch the breath that kept shaking out of his chest, and his feet bounced off the floor in an irregular rhythm, jarring his entire body.

Through his thick fleshy eyes, he looked into the smoky mirror above the coat rack, witnessing the strange blur of his physical body, the smoothing of his fissured face and crinkled skin, and the way he appeared now to be both matter and spirit. Then the cracked corners of his thin lips rose, and with deep joy, he cried out, "Deliverance!"

⌐ final acts ⌐

LOBBING THE LAST SANDBAG to Nick Archer, Bill Dunleavy declares, "That's it. We're through."

Nick smiles broadly, tosses the last bag onto the sandwall, and slicks back his rain-soaked hair. He nails a high five against Bill's palm and rushes off— sprinting through the soccer field, then vaulting over its cyclone fence and landing gracefully in the high school parking lot.

Bill cranes his neck, trying to track Nick's circuitous route through the crowded courtyard. He envies the young man's assured choreography, his quick zigzagging through clusters of people who huddle near the Red Cross van, his effortless hoisting of Tommy Nichols for a piggyback ride.

Then he sees Nick's path end at the gymnasium entrance where Helen Cantor awaits. Even in his faraway location at the perimeter of the school grounds, he is pierced by her radiant response with Nick's arrival. The reflexive bitterness he feels exposes his hostile outlook toward anyone who appears to be happy. And yet, when he closes his eyes to end further witness of the couple's toxic joy, he sees Maddy's face aglow in the warm light cast from a Bunsen burner flame during their chem class many years ago.

Thunder echoes throughout the canyon, and gusty winds pitch salvoes of horizontal rain. Bill opens his eyes, and a painful spectacle enters his view: Nick and Helen huddling on the steps, their arms entwined.

He knows it is unconscionable, but, still, he must admit what he genuinely desires—for something to disabuse them of their unbridled joy. Something to teach them that they will not be invincible forever or immune to time's degradations.

Pacing along the sandwall he has helped to build, he tries to quell his mounting agitation. It is hard to believe that, after hours of intensive labor, still, he has not adequately discharged his dark energy. To make matters worse, his flask has been empty all day, and lukewarm coffee is all that the Red Cross van has to offer. He feels so contrary, he imagines tearing down the sandwall and inviting the Baptista in. Anger floods him, surging forth from a depthless internal spring. He throws his flask into the floodwaters that stealthily inch up the sandwall. A lurching wind delivers aerial drifts of pesticides and fertilizers. The school tower bell clangs, and Bill shouts beneath the din, "What the fuck am I doing here?"

Sirens sound, but the only peril he senses is internal. Increasingly, his hands tremble. His mind obsesses over whiskey and the festering regrets that it usually tames. Raindrops burrow under the collar of his yellow slicker and mingle with cold sweat breaking across his chest.

He forces himself to think about something other than his physical discomfort. And his mind automatically alights on a memory of standing in this same location on the outskirts of the school. It is September 12, 2001, the day after the World Trade Center attacks. Everyone in Woodhaven had been drawn by communal spirit to gather inside the gymnasium. Ella had prepared a program, the Podroskis supplied pastries, and Norma provided sodas from the bar. Carlos sang the national anthem, and Raj delivered a speech that advocated peace and tolerance. Still, all the while, Bill remained outside—wondering then, as he wonders now, whether he'd ever belong to the community he has never been able to leave.

While impassively noting a breach in the sandwall through which water trickles, he considers his life as one long and dreary sequence of personal failings. One terrible mistake after another, each less original in the making. He remembers privately daring his first wife to leave, and how it took her two long years before finally asking for the divorce. He recalls her dumbfounded look as she walked out the door, still without the answers she sought from him. But he could not explain his sullen withdrawal or infidelity. Because all he had understood himself, from his deepest internal accounting, was that he needed her to wound him and leave him in a state of longing and regret.

Lightning slices the sky above midcanyon, and rain bleeds down. The bell tower releases another deep-throated hum that lingers in the air. Now he returns to his conversation with Ella during last year's Fourth of July parade. She had pulled him aside and forcibly set him down on a bench, warning him that he'd never find peace by "pumping whiskey into his blood." He laughed all the while she tried to pry the flask from his hand. He rolled his eyes when she asked, "Why are you so incapable of feeling joy, even when it's surrounding you?" When she claimed that his troubles came from the bottle—not from his family or the community he's always belittled—he just shook his head. And whenever she pointed to evidence of the good in his life, he only saw grief and disappointment. He viewed his purported "thriving farm" as a mocking substitute for the golf course franchise he had always hoped to manage. His "loving mother and father," long dead, were responsible for his suffocating entrapment in Woodhaven. And he knew that his apparent "good health" was mere fragile defiance against his relentlessly self-destructive drinking. Finally, while sweeping out an arm to indicate all the townspeople parading by, Ella said, "Most people feel blessed to be living in our proud town." Still, all he could manage was to marvel at his neighbors' marching children in their Wal-Mart best, wondering how long it would take for them to realize that the main street in most other towns stretched longer than one block.

BILL RETURNS HIS ATTENTION to the courtyard and anxiously scans for Maddy and Ed. The hours spent sandwalling had been an eternity of waiting to find out whether they survived. He is as fearful of finding them as he is afraid that he won't. And while the anxiety helps to subdue his rage, it also refuels his feelings of shame and cowardice. Still, the chance to see them provides his only hope of being freed from his interminable unhappiness. And while he cannot undo what he did to them so many years ago, telling them the overdue truth might free them from the damaging falsehoods of his making.

Privately, for the millionth time, he admits his responsibility for Maddy's accident and the deaths of her parents and aunt. He obsessively recounts his foolish misdeeds: had he not tinkered with the Bertollis' car, the brakes would not have failed. The car would have stopped in time, and no one would have drowned in the Baptista. Had he left the car alone—as Ed had instructed—Maddy would have lived free of the injuries and losses for which he is to blame.

"If only . . ." he says aloud, thinking about the afternoon that grabs him daily by the throat. An otherwise perfect Saturday, May 1970, just two weeks before Woodhaven High's prom. Warm breezes carried lavender and jasmine from the West Ridge hills, and a winning Giants game played on the radio. The sun shone brilliantly, and the skinny creek meandering off the Baptista shimmered like Christmas tinsel. Ed had taken a break at the bakery and left him with two explicit instructions: to mind the gas pump and change the oil in the Bertollis' car.

But it had been difficult to bridle his enthusiasm after Mr. Bertolli dropped off the car minutes earlier. All the while they had talked, Bill had struggled to keep quiet his plan to invite Maddy to the prom during Monday's chem class, thinking she should be first to hear. Instead, he talked excitedly with Mr. Bertolli about golf swings, the ballgame, and the road trip the Bertolli family was going to take the next morning.

Still, after dutifully replacing the oil and filter in the Bertollis' car, Bill couldn't stop staring obsessively at it—a flawless white '65 Rambler Marlin, eight-cylinder fastback hardtop. Finally yielding to compulsion, he opened the door and peered inside. Instantly, he was intoxicated by the lingering scent of Maddy's Nina Ricci perfume, and he breathed it in longingly. Then he sat in the driver's seat, imagining Maddy at his side, the two of them traveling to places they'd never been. He fingered a quarter that he found on the floor, envisioning Maddy having held it before.

He exited the car and popped its hood. He examined the engine which still felt warm. After checking the hoses, he topped off the fluid tanks and tamped down a slack red wire. He washed the windows and shined the hubcaps. Then he grabbed Ed's toolbox and dolly, and he slid underneath the car. He tried to identify all the parts of the car's underbelly as he had learned from Ed. He tightened some bolts and screws, cleaned a few gears, and tested various cables from their beginning to end

On Tuesday—two days after the Bertollis' accident—he showed up for his after-school shift at Ed's. He'd been sleepless the night before, with his mind obsessively circling around his guilt. He could not stop imagining the Bertollis' car crashing into a guardrail, and Maddy catapulting through the air. The horror kept replaying—the car sliding off Berringer's Bridge, Maddy's parents and aunt drowning in the Baptista. And he kept hearing it all, too—the collision, the skid, the screams and moans.

He was startled to find Ed waiting for him at the garage. And even more startled when Ed outright asked, "Bill, did you fiddle with the Bertollis' car on Saturday?"

Bill discovered in that moment that, while it was excruciating to consider lying to Ed, it was more excruciating to tell him the truth. Looking directly into Ed's knowing eyes, he denied having tinkered with the car. He claimed only to have changed the oil and filter—as he'd been instructed.

Ed said nothing. But through a wordless mutual understanding, he turned away and Bill walked out the door.

Afterwards, Ed's spirit wore down over time under the weight of public speculation about his culpability in the tragedy. And Bill took refuge in taking over his family's farm, which he had steadfastly despised.

BRANCH-BENDING WINDS disperse loose sand and shake nettles from trees. Bill knows he should seek protection, but that would require him to join all the people inside the shelter. Besides, he is paralyzed by shame and self-loathing, realizing that, by abandoning Maddy in her cabin today, he has again left her alone in a perilous condition that he helped to create.

Then someone calls out his name. He looks toward the courtyard and sees Norma and Juliette beckoning to him. But he returns a dismissive gesture and remains near the sandwall, waiting for them to give up their efforts.

After they do, he rescans the courtyard in search of Maddy and Ed. Rain patters the ground like the offbeat ticking of a tired clock.

But then Ella appears by the soccer field gate. Pressing her husband's police scanner to one ear, she waves vigorously to Bill, repeatedly calling his name.

Still, he stands firmly on the opposite side of the enormous chasm that separates him from Ella, him from everyone in Woodhaven, him from the world. And when he does not move toward her, she places her hands on her hips and shakes her head.

But just when he thinks that he will be left deservedly alone, she makes a beeline toward him. He is shocked to see her approach, wondering how she could be so oblivious to the impassable divide between them. Still, she moves toward him like a muscular missionary, without doubt or fear.

Realizing that she won't be turning back, Bill begins to worry. He braces himself against the formidable force of Ella's zeal to save him.

But then she stops suddenly, and her expression changes, reflecting intense attention to her police scanner. Meanwhile, a crowd rushes toward the soccer field. Lightning cracks once, twice, three times. The courtyard loudspeakers announce urgent but indecipherable messages. Ella looks quizzically up to the sky. The air buzzes, trees vibrate.

Bill internalizes the overwhelming external commotion. He looks yearningly to cheering crowds who line up along the soccer field fence, generating vitalizing currents that pass directly into him. A helicopter hovers above to which people point. Ella signals again to Bill, and, this time, she draws him in. A commanding force urges him toward her and the crowd, and he begins to move inexorably toward them. Screaming wide-eyed children jump up and down. The Red Cross medics rush a gurney through the gate. A collective cheer erupts when the helicopter begins its descent. Rainfall pours from the sky like baptismal water, and Bill finds himself running toward the helicopter, seeing that it carries Maddy whose bent hand presses open against the window.

⌐ natural law ⌐

FOR DAYS, I'VE BEEN AT THE EPICENTER of countless personal tragedies.

And, as Sheriff, I've had to force my neighbors and friends out of their homes and off their land. I've dredged the Baptista for bodies, and even carried out corpses of some people I've known. Up-close and personal, I've witnessed so much suffering from this flood, one person or family at a time.

And though the rains have stopped and the water has dropped below flood stage, already the finger-pointing's begun. People here are blaming the flood on whomever and whatever they can. On climate change and wayward Pacific storms. On grape growers and winery owners for throwing up berms on upstream properties. On the utility board for keeping too much water in the reservoir and then having to open its floodgate during the storms. They blame flash floods for flashing, mudslides for sliding. They fault fate, god, the weather service . . .

I have a reputation for being a sturdy lawman, and I hail from a family of distinguished military officers. But coming up against this flood took a big toll on me. And I needed a different perspective to help me depersonalize all the agony.

So, I stole a private moment in the helicopter and took a solo flight over Thalburg canyon. And I got what I needed—a bird's eye view of our Armageddon, unmediated by my neighbors' sorrows.

What I saw—that the Baptista was neither cruel nor virtuous. It wasn't ugly or beautiful, damning or redemptive. And it didn't care about anyone in particular—their children or parents, their crops or cars, their chickens or photographs.

The river was an indifferent god coursing through our lives. It was simply nature, existing in its unknowable and ungovernable ways, confounding everything I thought I knew.

Acknowledgments

I began writing these fictional stories about people confronting a devastating flood while I was receiving cancer chemotherapy in the late '90s. I drafted the first story, wondering how or whether I would survive the dark flood pressing against my own life. And I kept writing. More stories involving more characters materialized, each adding a new dimension of the flood to an ever-widening perspective.

I am deeply grateful to my friends and family who kept me afloat during my flood years and made me laugh—especially Diane Buczek, Norma Scannell, Michelle Paymar, Véronique Martinaud, Jean Kaufman, Terri Rubinstein, Andrée Abecassis, Leslie Martin, Joan King-Angell, and Bingo.

And for their vital encouragement along the way, I thank Marcia Childress, Marilyn Frye, Tom Tuttle, Max McMillen, Frederique DeLacoste, Ella Riter, Felice Newman, Dan Hatfield, and Susan Riter.